Love across a broken map

Short Stories from The Whole Kahani

First published 2016 by Dahlia Publishing Ltd
6 Samphire Close Hamilton
Leicester LE5 1RW
ISBN 9780956696786

Abridged versions of the following stories were previously broadcast on BBC Radio 4: 'Three Singers' by Kavita A. Jindal, 'We Are All Made of Stars' by Rohan Kar and 'Naz' by Iman Qureshi.

Printed and bound by Grosvenor Group

A CIP catalogue record for this book is available from The British Library

CONTENTS

Foreword
SUSMITA BHATTACHARYA

This year I have been concentrating on reading short stories, especially collections from the South Asian diaspora. There are two reasons for this: one is that I want to engage with the #readdiverse2016 and read widely and as diverse as possible. And the second reason, as I belong to the same category of 'writer of South Asian background', I want to see what is being published, and learn what is the trend in publishing stories from these diverse backgrounds.

I was honoured to be invited to write a foreword for this eclectic mix of short fiction. I found myself going back to my favourite Neil Gaiman's quote as I spent my afternoons, sitting in the sunshine, and getting completely absorbed in these stories: "Short stories are tiny windows into other worlds and other minds and other dreams. They are journeys you can make to the far side of the universe and still be back in time for dinner."

Though the writers of this collection are of British Asian background that may be the only reference we have to South Asian culture. These stories do not fall back on the stereotypical issues that we expect in stories, films, etc... to do with the British Asian or South Asian culture. There are no forced marriages, arranged marriages, domestic violence, culture-gap issues in this collection. What we do have are darker characters, stories that are gritty, bold, funny and without the stereotype.

I found the anthology to be very character driven, and each of the characters felt very special. Dimmi Khan's *Rocky Romeo* is a gigolo, but he hates 'the touch of flesh, the way women tried to cover him with their hands, possess him'. He prefers the anonymity of cybersex, until one woman starts to get under his skin. There are stories of burgeoning love, extra-marital love, obsessive love and also the inability to love. The story of Peony and Anjali, in *Watermelon Seeds* by C.G. Menon, reflects on young infatuation, experimenting with love and heartbreak, while in Iman Qureshi's *Naz*, a terrifying Staffordshire bull terrier called Doris brings together two unlikely lovers. On the subject of unlikely partners, *We Are All made of Stars* by Rohan Kar, brings together in arranged matrimony a young Englishman and an Indian woman, but why does he agree to marry in a tradition quite alien to him? Suman Bakshi finds herself obsessed with a writer she has never met, until one day she does and things do not look good from the start in *Soul Sisters* by Reshma Ruia.

The stories are a collection from a London based group of fiction writers of South Asian origin, The Whole Kahani, and its aim is 'to give a new voice to old stories and increase the visibility of South Asian writers in Britain.' A couple of these stories have been previously broadcast on BBC Radio 4 'Introductions', where they are described as to be exploring 'what it means to be mixed race, the tensions between modern independence and family traditions, and the impact of really going it alone in the face of family expectations.'

These stories remind me of my own writing journey, when I started out I was influenced by my favourite short fiction writer, Jhumpa Lahiri. I loved her style, but at that time, I accepted the themes of her stories: of immigration and homesickness, of second generation conflict to be the themes to write about as a South Asian writer. It helped me hone my skills as a writer, but it challenged me to push the boundaries further. Explore beyond the familiar, or what was expected of me. It made me go beyond what felt comfortable, and the stories in this collection have achieved just that. When talking about her writing process for a short story in the O. Henry Prize collection, Alice Munro says of *What Do You Want To Know For?* that it was the only story she had ever written that was 'hardly a story'. That 'from the beginning to the end, it happened.' I'd like to think that this is how new writing from South Asian writers will be perceived. Not expecting the usual exotic ingredients, but making the ordinary happen. The last story in the collection, *By Hand* by Farrah Yusuf is very Munroesque in the way the story unfolds. Seemingly nothing happens, but there are many layers within the story that start to peel away, eventually leading us into its heart.

This collection invites us to roam through the lives and loves of these characters, inhabit their thoughts, laugh or cry with them, or bite our lips with frustration. And for sure, I found myself struggling to put the book down and to return to the present in time to prepare dinner!

Watermelon Seeds

C. G. MENON

Peony has whiskers; she has a pointy face and a tail made out of blue raffia; she's messing about in boats and dabbling-up-tails-all, and I am in love.

'You have to say 'Blow spring-cleaning!' now, Anjali,' she insists, and jumps with a splash of patent-leather shoes right into the tricky, rippling flood that swirls down the gutter between our houses. The monsoon is coming, and the water will soon be ankle-deep and silted up with rotting fruit. But Peony and I don't care because by then we'll be inside, watching a Cantonese soap opera on her drawing-room television and eating fried watermelon seeds. She'll crack one open between her teeth and I'll taste it a split-second before she swallows, because Peony and I are two-together like dots on a domino and everything we feel is the same.

We were given our parts for the school play today; it was chatter-and-elbows in front of the notice-board, it was congratulations waved off; – *so much fuss, lah! all talk-talk* – and tears in the padang outside the school gate. I'm an understudy for Mole, but Peony, oh, Peony is going to be Ratty and how could anyone not be in love? Mr and Mrs Wong will come to watch her in the dark school gym with the fans spinning high up in the rafters where you can only reach if you climb one-two-feet-together up a plaited rope in your gym skirt. They will sit on the folding metal chairs,

1

and the spotlights will glint off their spectacles and mosquitoes will bite at their ankles, and none of this will matter because their daughter is Ratty in a river of light on stage, and this is where it all begins.

'Prompt me again, Anjali!' She reaches out for my hand and tugs me into the water too. My hands fold warm into hers and my feet bump up against her toes, and for a moment our faces float frail as ghosts somewhere below the water. And then she kicks up a giant spray, a fan of rainbow drops that soaks my dress and leaves her slumped solid and giggling against me.

'I won't play!' But I will, of course, and she pulls me up on the mud-splashed gutter to dangle my feet next to hers in the stream.

'Blow spring-cleaning...?' I offer tentatively. Her face splits into a wide, wide smile as she sails into her lines and I think my heart breaks, just a little bit, because now Peony is Ratty again. This is our last day before the holidays and I want to save every little bit of it, to squeeze it up tight in my hands.

'Come and watch tv with me, Anjali,' she says as she steps toe-heel out of her shoes on the shallow steps of the Wong's verandah. A stone lion guards the door, and I stroke its face, already blurred from years of our hugs. The hall behind it smells of silence; of lilies and rosewater and cool polished wood, and Peony disappears down it like a breath against the wind. Next door, my own quiet house reeks of coconut oil and turmeric. *Such a Tamil smell*, Mrs Wong said once when she thought we were upstairs, and for months after that Peony and I mouthed *Tamil-smell* across the classroom to each other when we got our homework wrong.

'I have to pack first,' I call to the fluttering lace of her dress. A breeze is coming down from the jungle and everything is alive with it. Along the padang the casuarina leaves are rustling and the soft petals of hibiscus are being slowly shredded. All through Kuala Lipis hair-ribbons will be whipping and sarongs will be blowing, and everyone will know the monsoon is on its way from the polished pewter sky.

Peony turns at the end of the hall and calls back something rude in Cantonese. She's taught me a little and I know that these are bad words; grown-up words to reach into the future and pull the years and everything that waits in them tumbling down like a stack of dominoes onto her tangled black head. But then a silver curtain of rain sweeps down from the road and her skirt flutters in the dark of the hall and Peony is gone.

#

'Here, sir-madam. Colonial House.' The driver glances back at us, glued tight as snails on the lumpish leather seats. His hair leaves a coconut oil smear on the back of his seat.

'Already we paid so no money now, ok lah?' My mother grabs at the back of his seat, smearing the hair-oil over her fingers (Tchee! So dirty!), and levers herself up from her mushroom of skirts and travelling rugs.

'Hello! Hello!' my father calls. 'Come and help us unload.' He slaps at his arms in a bluff and hearty way I don't recognise, as though somewhere on the journey someone has slipped a different Appa into our car. The verandah gate opens and a bearded fleet of uncles and uncles-by-marriage begin to steam up like full-bellied sailing ships.

'Out you get, little Anjali; lock, stock and barrel.' The uncles are like this, I remember, full of mysterious phrases with the sense sucked out of them. Barrels mean rum, I think, and pirates and fifteen men on a dead man's chest. *Tamil-smell uncles*, I whisper, but Peony is miles away back home with the watermelon seeds and the tumbling monsoons and nobody hears me. I slide down flat in my seat until my bare knees joggle the seat in front, and listen to an uncle drop our bags plump-plump on the ground.

'Come on, Anjali!'

Behind that verandah is my grandfather's house, and behind that are the courtyards. They stretch out like a rope of caves, each of them darker than the next and filled with banyan trees and swamps and bricked-up wells. The window-shutters are open upstairs and I can see the faces of my cousins, crammed in like mice in a nest. Each year they arrive before us, stepping lordly off the plane from England instead of being lock-stock-barrelled out of a station taxi. They leave a sort of silt wherever they go – hair-ties, and pencil shavings and faded perfume – and for the next two weeks I will pick my way through this in the spaces that are left.

A door slams inside, and then the aunties troop kajal-eyed out onto the verandah, bulging from their saris and warm as cats from an afternoon nap. Amma begins to shuffle from her seat, muttering the complaints she's been saving in her throat for their loving ears, and I follow all alone like a single dot on a domino.

#

'Girls, take Anjali with you today. I'm sure she knows some new games.' My cousins and I swap silent, muttering glances over our breakfast-plates. *How-can-**she**-know-anything*, and *Leave-me-alone*, and underneath all that a sort of awkward *it's-not-your-fault-though*, like bumping elbows with a friend in the dark.

'If she wants to, Mummy.' Priya is the oldest girl-cousin; she's fifteen and poised forever between the children and the kajal-aunties. I wonder if she likes this, or if she's too old for all this 'liking-disliking', as my mother would say, and is therefore truly grown-up. Priya has a lovely faint smile, and a whitish face like ivory gone yellow; her voice is smooth and English and everything she says is the exact opposite of what she means.

I stare down at my Weetabix and don't say anything. There's a spoonful of Nutella on top, dolloped there by one of the aunties who doesn't know that Nutella is only for treats. I've been saving it for the final mouthful, but now Priya's words are hanging in the air, and everything is melting into plain brown mush. Anjali, don't be such a baby, someone will say in a moment, and then the Weetabix will stick in my throat and Nutella will never be a treat again.

'She can come with me.' Rahul says suddenly, and I look up in surprise. Rahul is thirteen and right in the middle of the boy-cousins. He has eyelashes like splashes of ink and slabbed front teeth too big for his mouth, and I want both those things too, with a kind of fierce and determined itch. Peony likes him, though she's only ever seen photographs, and begs me to tell her about him every year. She said once in Truth-or-Dare that she would marry him when she grew up, and I refused to play anymore until she took it back.

'If you like,' I mutter into my bowl, and swirl the milk around until Amma scolds and snatches it away, Nutella and Weetbix and baby-and-all.

#

'Are you going to play cricket?' I ask.

Rahul and the boy-cousins have stamped a pitch into the biggest courtyard, and out there they take turns to be heroes; Viv Richards, and Peter Willey and others whose names I've never even heard. I don't get to be a hero though, only a comic side-kick Anjali trailing after dropped catches and missed throws while jackfruit blossom drops on her head. I whisper one of Peony's rude words under my breath, and Rahul peers at me.

'No, I'm going to show you something. Come on, Anjali - quickly!'

He takes me through the courtyards to the furthest one, where durian trees mass together and banyans choke the walls. It looks like a place from the horror movies Peony and I watched in Kuala Lipis; a swampy tangle where sharp-nailed ghosts and blood-sucking pontianaks shriek at night. The windows to the back bedrooms are high above us, and tonight our grandparents will mumble there safe in their mosquito-netted dreams. For now, though, the shutters droop open in the sun, half-hidden by slack jowls of bougainvillea, and a banyan tree looms nearby. Its bare branches swoop down to make a dim cave speckled with shadows and the tiny smells of the naked earth.

I put my hands on my hips, where the waist of m y new dress ties. It's blue cotton with ruffles, and the feel of the satin sash makes me brave. 'I don't see anything,' I say.

Rahul doesn't answer, but instead squats down and begins to scoop out a shallow trench. It criss-crosses the ground, a glistening gutter of slug-slime and earth that doubles back just beyond my toes. I think I hear the pontianaks hissing from the banyan roots and beating at its banks, then Rahul sits back on his heels with a look of triumph.

'There!' He wipes his hands clean on a patch of moss. 'It's going to be a house, Anjali. Don't you see?'

And suddenly, there it is. I crouch down next to Rahul and the ditches turn into walls, and beyond them are halls and rooms and endless jewelled courtyards where nobody will ever leave me out of games again. The pontianaks can cry all they like, and the cousins can burrow like mice, but this is mine - all mine - and inside here I will choose how everything turns out.

Rahul's left a gap for the front door where a mass of fungus has spread and blistered, and I slide my shoes off heel-toe. He's forgotten to draw steps, but I climb them anyway and pat the empty place by the door-gap where my stone lion will be. 'Blow spring-cleaning,' I mutter, and from somewhere my skirt flutters in a breeze and there's a silver scent of rain.

#

'Anjali! So dirty, your feet! Ai-yoh, do you think I'm coming here to wash and slave for you?' Amma is upset, or she wouldn't talk like that; not like she does at home. When we're at my grandfather's house she tries to speak nicely-nicely, like the English aunties.

'It was my fault, Aunt Sajni. We were playing in the courtyards.' Rahul's voice is smooth as pebbles underwater, and it soothes Amma. She nods her head one-two-three along with all the other kajal-aunties who loll on kitchen chairs sipping mango juice and watching us eat. Amma nestles back into the middle of them, and her bite melts down to a purr of complaint somewhere deep in her plump dark neck.

Rahul beckons me over to the sideboard, where he's heaping a plate full of the soft white mounds of idli. He squeezes them together so they bulge like bosoms; fleshy like Amma or the big girls at school, and I start to giggle.

When Priya takes one, his fingers brush against mine and a little smile slinks between us, like a silver firefly in the deep-green dining room.

#

After lunch Rahul and I wander outside, stranded and small in the beating bronze air. Everything is silent, and even the cats lie exhausted and slit-eyed in puddles of tar-black shade. Upstairs the girl-cousins are lying down too, in their vests and knickers with their strange white bodies beached beneath the mosquito nets. Like slugs, I tell Rahul, and when he laughs it fizzes cold and clear in my head.

In the durian courtyard the trees look baked, crisp and curled tight in the heat. I've been telling Rahul about our play; about Anjali-the-Mole and Peony-the-Ratty; about the stone lion I've hugged every morning before school; about the monsoon and the watermelon seeds and how Peony and I will one day be actors under the clear yellow sun in California. I don't think he's listening, but then he remembers to walk up our invisible steps and pat our stone lion, and I forgive him.

'We need a guest room, Anjali,' he tells me, and I immediately start to squabble with him, in a comforting sort of way that I know doesn't really matter. A guest room has to have flowers, I insist, and he offers to climb the banyan tree where orchids clump above our heads, but I refuse. He has to creep back to the house, I tell him, and steal some fresh-cut flowers from my grandmother's vases. He mustn't be seen, and he must double back to confuse his tracks, and stay downwind of the aunties to avoid being captured. His eyes gleam as he listens and his teeth shine wet, and for one moment I'm two-together again, and it feels disloyal and lovely.

While Rahul's gone I draw in our steps and our stone lion. Its face is sharp and its eyes are crossed, all the better to look both ways with. The soil must be damp, because a pool collects under my feet as I draw and soon my feet are wet from the squelching mud and mosquitoes are swarming beneath the lion's fur.

#

It's dusk by the time Rahul comes back. The sun slants gold through the vines, and glosses off the banyan leaves in a sunset haze. A cricket gives a tinny little chirrup, but the noise cuts off with a stutter of alarm as Rahul pushes back.

He's brought flowers from every vase in the house and they drip cool on my fingers, smooth and waxy and smelling of rosewater. *Stolen flowers for you, Anjali*, he says, and comes to sit next to me with his back against the garden wall. His arm is damp against mine and I watch a mosquito land under his ear, on that thumb patch of bare salt skin. A red lump starts to swell, but he's fiddling with the flower stems and doesn't notice, so for one moment there's a tiny secret about him that belongs just to me.

'There!' He passes me the flowers, plaited into a twining bouquet, and asks, 'Will Peony be our first guest?'

I'd forgotten all about the guestroom and I swallow. The flowers are wilting from being plaited, and their colours have already faded a little in the dry night air. Rahul slaps at his ear and says 'Mosquito bite!' in a tone of surprise, and my secret is gone.

'I don't want Peony here,' I tell him and the pontianaks and devils nod one-two-three and purr down in their throats. 'She wants to - ' and now it's almost too late, and then one breath later I take his hand and then it is too late. 'She wants to *marry* you.'

There's a pause, a heartbeat where nothing moves. His face is a glow of ivory in the dusk, and his ink-splash eyelashes are blinking soft as a breath. And then he spins around, and the air is thick with tiger-striped shadows; with the choking smell of durian and the sound of Rahul laughing.

I push him away and he whoops with a metallic sort of jeer, bitter like teeth on tinfoil.

'You're in love!'

He's found it out and the secret's too big to keep to himself. It bites at his lips and squeals for air and the next moment it's sent him cackling like a dart right into the knot of cousins somewhere outside. His feet scuff our fragile walls and his sandal-thumps echo down our hallways and rooms.

When he's gone, when it's quiet and all the normal day-coloured sounds have come shuffling back, I lean against the garden wall. I whisper rude words in Cantonese under my breath and with the very tip of one finger I make a little trench around me, just enough to keep out the tiniest pontianak and the slowest devil.

#

Back at school, Peony still has her raffia tail; she still has her whiskers and her pointy face; she's still messing-about-in-boats, and for her, everything is still the same.

I don't look at her during class, and when the bell goes I stay in the classroom until she leaves, looking back at me in a puzzled sort of way as though she, too, doesn't understand how it's all turned out. I don't tell her about the durian courtyard, or the pontianaks or the way those chants of *Anjali's in love, Anjali's in love* braided themselves through my cousins' sing-song games. I take somebody else as my partner for gym class, and we climb one-two so high up a plaited rope that I think I might never come down again. And later, I give up my role in the school play, and tell the drama teacher that Amma refused to let me join.

The night of the performance, I sit on my bedroom floor with the light off and a mosquito coil glowing under the bed. I watch cockroaches scuttle along the door-frame and breathe in Tamil-smell and whisper 'Bother spring-cleaning' into the gloom. But perhaps I get the timing wrong, because over in the school hall Peony forgets her lines, and cries in the chalk-and-paint wings of the gymnasium stage.

Peony and I will never speak again, except for brief words with their tails caught sharp between our teeth. She will move to Kuala Lumpur to study drama, and when my mother rings to tell me about this I will pretend to have heard already. By then I will be in England, and not long afterwards I will marry an Englishman with pale white skin and hair the colour of sand. Our children will be fair as ivory, and their teachers will call me Angie; our house will smell only of floral air-freshener and my husband will, in any case, dislike turmeric.

And then, on those short summer nights when the air feels like home, I will slide my slippers off heel-toe and creep downstairs. I will find a Cantonese film on the television, while my sandy husband sleeps off his Sunday-night stew and the children lie beached under the drape of blankets. The heroine will smile out at me from the dark, and I will taste the watermelon seeds between her teeth, but she will never be Peony, not ever, and by then I won't understand a single word she says.

Rocky Romeo
DIMMI KHAN

Rocky begins with the shirt. He lets his fingers tease the silk, the visceral thrill of material against skin, imagines how it will feel, when he slips it on and off. The label, on the collar, satisfies, the price tag is checked.

The scent is next, he picks it up on the air, veers towards it. The top of the aftershave tester is cold against his wrist, as he dabs, sniffs, turns the whisky style bottle and memorises the name. He makes a note of the cost.

Two senses ablaze, he searches for something to enliven his ocular realm.

Silver bracelet, lock of opal and amethyst. Bling, bling. He asks to try, it fits and sits, it's his, he must possess it.

Satisfied, Rocky pulls his shoulders back, unburdened by the pressure to buy, leaves the shop. Empty handed.

A memory outside the entrance, stuffing bread and cans of beans into his duffle coat. Too young at three to know what was being done to him, an expert by six.

Rocky breathes it out, lets the thoughts travel into the distance of his mind, getting fainter, until they are small and grey and can't hurt him.

The sun is stirring up dust, sweat, people, as they cram onto Oxford Street. Rocky sits at a café, sipping hot chocolate, tapping the calories in to his daily tracker app. He watches the mass of bodies, safe with his terrace view. He continues to swipe, drum, slide, his fingers caressing his phone's screen.

He recalls the labels, the prices, adds links to where they can be purchased. Adds comments, what the material objects mean to him, how much the purchaser would mean to him.

Rocky's facial from the morning is still fresh, so he takes a selfie, adds it to his collection. Sends it to a couple of special women, gets himself printed onto their busy days, see which one will bite.

The waitress is from Plovid, Bulgaria's second city she tells him. It has a Roman Amphitheatre, an Ottoman Mosque, cobbled streets, an easy pace. She has milk white skin, bright grey eyes, auburn hair, neat waist, curves. Rocky is unmoved.

He has praised damaged, self-loathing, too many times. His play acting, learning to love imperfection, has ironically left him with a love for it. The raw, natural beauty of the waitress, is as flat as a magazine image to Rocky.

Still, he flirts with Albena, as she pours her life story into his eyes. Practice when he can.

She tells him she misses her father, her mother has died.

Rocky is taken unawares, flinches. A father to miss, he envies Albena. His own left him with a black slick of criminal experience, and a lifetime in care.

A hell of a lot more than his mother ever did though.

He leaves Albena a huge tip. Envy burns inside him, as he walks away thinking of her father.

Rocky lets his body open into a hot bath, aromas of amber and musk steam against the tiles. His muscles separate under his skin, as he stretches, yogi like. Busy day, busier night ahead.

His phone tells him he has a text. He uses the sound of coins jingling in a pocket.

His soapy finger struggles with the phone's touchscreen, he wipes it on a towel, watches as the shirt shows up as bought.

Rocky logs into his profile, sees his gift list, sees what is left. The aftershave, the bracelet from that morning. A few minor items leftover from previous shopping sprees.

Rocky goes to the gifts purchased page, and sees which of his client's has bought him the shirt.

Monica. Mumbai socialite, heiress to jute furniture or plastic chappals, he can't remember. That's shoddy, he must look up her file. He takes a selfie of himself, his intimate parts hidden by soapy water. Wink, wink, grin, perfect teeth, biceps taut, a bit of tongue flicked out.

Monica calls. Rocky doesn't answer. Monica knows the drill.

Skype, one hour, a hundred pounds, via Paypal.

Rocky plays Monica's message.

'I need you jaan,' she says, breathless, desperate, strung out.

Horny housewife, philandering husband, nowhere to scratch that itch.

Rocky wonders if it's always a cliché if it's true?

Rocky isn't that sort of boy, he thinks with pride. First course only, whets the appetite, wets the women.

Rocky, unattainable, he feels his vanity, an ache in the groins, the drug they all want.

His stomach knots at the thought of drugs. Rocky remembers, aged six, having his stomach pumped. His father used him as a mule, a donkey, stuffing plastic bags of coke into Rocky's mouth, holding his nose till he swallowed.

'Your mother did one good thing, gave you her looks. You look like an angel. They will search the shit out of me, but you, they won't touch.'

They didn't, until a bag burst, and he started to vomit blood.

Jingle, jingle. The phone breaks into his self-pity, another notification.

The scent is purchased.

Raqib. Political heir to a Pakistani ruling dynasty, fast tracked through the judiciary, already looking at judgeship at thirty-two. Rocky lets the stab of jealousy dissipate, the success borne from a normal family. Instead he runs his wrist across his nose. The faint citrus of the aftershave from earlier still lingers.

Anonymous. Purdah.

It took time, weeks, months, years even. Rocky let them move at their own pace, reveal when they were clawing at the walls, craving him. And they all craved him, eventually. His mother's fine bone structure, his sculpted body. They all loved the shell, they all had a use for that. Just like his father.

Rocky didn't care, their fingerprints were never real, only virtual.

The melancholy violins dimmed as he was fostered, a childless couple with decades of pent up love to shower on him. They nurtured him, sent him to university. Then died in a car crash.

Rocky was heartbroken, broken, broke. He started off through cybersex, mutual pleasure. He hated the touch of flesh, the way women tried to cover him with their hands, possess him. One cyber stalker offered him money, said she would pay to watch him strip.

Rocky had been floating in sewage ever since.

One by one his friends, who had lauded him stud, player, da man, dropped off. Too nervous to have Rocky around their partners, didn't want him polluting their offspring.

Alone, lone, wolf. Rocky became his own cliché.

Sitara is logged on, her online status clear.

The sound of squelching, as Skype chats come at him. Women asking to speak to him, men asking him to strip. Rocky plays it dark, acts the busy boy, in demand, wait your turn.

Sitara.

The poet.

'My dignity is trampled, my honour is scorched. Melt into me, bring me to life again.'

Rocky remembers the first time, the first shayari. It was all he knew of her.

She doesn't indulge him in gifts, she pays him for his time.

'Don't switch your camera on,' she had said.

Her camera was switched off. Rocky unable to use his shell, forced to engage mentally, emotionally, spiritually.

At first she only typed her words. Slowly, as Rocky's heart turned wistful, as he shed tears for the beauty of them, he persuaded her to speak to him.

'They say the pen is sharper, they say the sword is blunt against my soul. When they took my lover, I watched as the sword cut his flesh. What use were my stories then?'

'You wrote his fable, gave him eternity,' Rocky had said. Sitara had gasped, switched off her Skype, her session ended forty minutes too soon.

Rocky had waited for hours, until the dawn cleaved the sky in two, desperate for her to return. He wanted to hear her gasp again, he craved her, needed her.

Understanding fell like burning stars, broke his world, as he tasted his own bitter poison.

'You free?' she types.

'Yes,' his response immediate.

'Check your account,' she types.

Rocky doesn't bother, she never fails to pay.

Rocky video calls, leaves his camera on. She drops the call. He calls again, camera off.

'Did you get the money ok?' she says.

Her body, her face, nothing more than a black rectangle.

'Yes,' he says. 'Sorry, about the video call. I've got nothing to hide from you though. Why won't you look at me? I'm dressed and decent.'

'They sit among whores, and talk of decency,' she says.

'Ouch,' he says.

'I didn't mean...does the moon dim when it sails over your house? Then why do you doubt your worth?'

Rocky pulls his sheets close around him, dims his light. Shame burns his face, he wants to be better for her, purer.

'Still, there is truth, and there is pain,' she says.

'My truth, but I'm not...that,' he says.

'Does it matter?' she says.

'Yes. Your opinion matters,' he says.

'I am nothing. I am not even a shadow. You walk over dust more valuable than me.'

She is gone, her words ache his heart. It forgets to beat.

The shirt arrives. It stays unopen.

The aftershave arrives. Rocky puts it away.

The bracelet is bought. Monica has purchased his time. He owes her.

For the first time in more time than he can recall, Rocky feels it's a chore, he feels it's wrong. This is not love, this is not sex, this is not lust. This is something grimier, grimmer.

His misery dissipates in his actions, as he Skypes with Monica, his shirt off, his hands carelessly touching himself, as she looks on. She fills his head with idle gossip, tells him money is to her like air, she has no concept of it.

She is rich, she wants him, in real time.

The bracelet arrives. It is cold metal, sharp stones.

Rocky sends Sitara a videocall.

She drops the call.

Rocky sends Sitara a videocall.

She drops the call.

They do the dance in the same parenthesis thirteen times.

Then she is gone.

He has no recourse.

He sits and he stares, and he wills for her to come back.

As the sun rises, he is deprived. Sleep, life, love, food, water. He is empty, and he is desperate.

Her words run through his head.

'The misery of your tyranny, is no less painful than death…'

The woman on the webcam is showing signs of a newbie. She laughs a lot, giggles, shy, touches her hair. It is black, touched with grey, falls to below her ears. The webcam has smoothed her lines, but those around her mouth are deep, he sees them. He imagines tracing them with his finger. Attraction to imperfection.

'I'm not sure what to do,' she says. 'Do you want me to do anything?'

No. He wants her to shut up, take her abashed embarrassment and leave.

'What do you feel like doing?' he says, revealing dimples as he smiles, touching his exposed collarbone.

'I like this…just chatting,' she says, giggling.

Giggle, giggle. Rocky feels nauseous.

Sitara is offline. Sitara is invisible.

Fuck her then. Fuck her and her purity, and her sanctimony, and her selfishness, and her privacy. She isn't so much better than him, she pays him for fuck's sake. His anger tastes sour, he swallows it back, and takes his shirt off.

'You're making me hot,' he says.

He rarely does this on a first date, prefers to keep them keen.

'Would you like me to play with myself for you?' he says.

He tries, but can't, gives up frustrated. The woman is understanding, compassionate, feels sorry for him. Rocky's failure has made him seem vulnerable. The woman is already falling in love with him.

'I hold you in my mind's eye, come and see, close your eyes, and look inside.'

Sitara's words, scratched into his head, like ancient hieroglyphs on stone caverns.

Rocky writes messages into space. He sends them, word after word, sentence after sentence. She will see them if she ever comes online. Maybe she is always online, she just hides herself? He blocked her the day before, deleted her. Only to add her again an hour later. The messages end with a simple statement: My life is in your hands. Come online or I die. He can't stop grinning, his threats have worked.

'I missed you,' he says.

'Pointless, this is nonsense, we are nothing. I am nothing, I am unreal,' she says.

'You are as real to me as the heart of a volcano,' he says. 'I want you. I will give this up, I will change myself for you. I want you to see me,' he says.

'No,' she says, she is quick, terse, instant.

'Yes,' he says, and he sends the video call. 'I have a blade, and it's flirting with a vein.' She accepts. Rocky sees himself in the corner of the screen. His small picture, in the bigger black rectangle that is her.

'I forgot my happiness, lost my desire…my soul found you, but did not know it was looking for you,' she says.

'Let me see you,' he says.

'There is no razor,' she says, but she doesn't drop the call.

'You already killed me,' he says. 'We can be happy.'

'I won't make any man happy, not now, not ever,' she says.

'What about me? You make me ecstatic.'

She is silent. Rocky's phone jingles, it is ignored.

'As I slope off into the sunrise, I can see the others already approaching your threshold,' she says.

'I don't want anyone else,' he says.

'You will, if you ever see me,' she says.

'Trust me,' he says.

She doesn't relent.

Rocky dismantles his life, client by client.

He takes down his website, he blocks his Skype contacts, he deletes his Paypal account, he takes the battery and SIM out of his phone.

The day is moulding itself from hazy light to wintry evening, but he opens his windows, letting the cold air brush through and cleanse his corners.

How did he get to this, how did this woman, faceless, strange, stranger, manipulate the master manipulator? Is that her strength, is that her power over him? No, it's so much simpler. She has loved Kabir, the boy he was, the man he wants to be, not Rocky, the malevolent parasite he is forced to be.

Kabir has been hiding, ignored, asleep. Sitara woke him, and now he won't let Rocky live in peace. He fills Rocky's head with chants of derision, a moral compass, tells him to stop feeling sorry for himself, showers him with disgust.

Rocky closes his eyes, and hears Kabir. He puts on loud music, runs as fast as he can, but Kabir is his heartbeat, his accelerated breathing, his blood.

Only Sitara calms him, only she lets Rocky be, because Kabir, invisible, unbidden, is loved by her. She bypassed the bricks and mortar, the funerary adornment, and touched the soul.

On the bed is a fresh blade. He wears a white shirt, leaves off the cufflinks, sits on his white bedspread. The blood will vibrate, its passion will be irrevocable, the result irreversible.

Sitara accepts his video call.

'I can't transfer the money,' she says, panic in her voice.

'I deleted my account,' he says.

'Why?'

'I gave it all up. For you.'

He rubs the blade between his thumb and forefinger, let's it cut the flesh, let's blood spot on his shirt, on the sheets. Kabir mocks him.

Rocky can turn screws, use subterfuge. For Sitara, the poet, a grand show, she will bite, she could have written this herself.

'What are you doing? Please stop,' Sitara says.

'Any last words? A poem to see me off?' Rocky says.

'Please, you can't, not for me, not ever...' she says.

'Let me see you,' he says.

'No,' she says.

He doesn't barter, he simply takes the blade to his wrist, his eyes lock into the black space that is her, and he begins to cut. Knowing he is hacking at skin, not a vein. Crimson rivulets stream across his hand. Better effects than he had planned.

For a second, a flicker, a fear, has he severed an artery by mistake? Why not, he soothes himself, why not go the way your father did, the way your life was headed. You don't deserve salvation, redemption. You don't deserve a mantle from the firmaments.

'Wait,' she says, terse, immediate.

The black rectangle that has been Sitara comes to life. Rocky watches as she fills the void. Her eyes are downcast, her lips trembling.

'You see now, how could anybody love this?'

Rocky is quiet, staring. His only urge is to reach out and touch her. Acting, playing the role too many times, imperfection is perfection for him.

'You are everything I want,' he says.

He puts the blade down, takes his shirt off, stems the blood, and touches the screen. She looks up at him, and he feels himself breathe for the first time in years.

Rocky is gone.

The Nine-Headed Ravan
RADHIKA KAPUR

She simply couldn't go on like this, she decided, on her twenty-fifth birthday. She had to know. The desire to know consumed her, invaded her mind like Mahmud of Ghazni invaded India.

They were at a restaurant by the beach. Anant had surprised her with a trip to Goa. When she got onto the bike at the bustling Greater Kailash market in Delhi, he said they were going to a restaurant, but drove to the airport instead. 'The restaurant is two hours away by flight,' he informed her with a wink.

'But, but, my clothes, my stuff!' she panicked.

'Just buy some there,' he said.

The flickering candles in grand candelabras, bunches of abundant, overflowing white lilies and the wooden floor of the restaurant that jutted into the ocean, turned the space into a magical fairyland. The sound of waves washing up against the shore and retreating soothed her ears. A Goan singer strummed his guitar to the tune of Ben King's *Stand by Me*. He laced his fingers with hers and said, 'I love you.' She squeezed his hand tight, but remained silent. It was neither the first time he had said it, nor the first time she didn't say it back. Anant looked at her and then away at the rolling, black sea. 'Will you ever say it?' he asked gently.

Later that night they made love. She felt cherished. It was a familiar feeling; one she felt every time their bodies came together. She felt the words, 'I love you.' She felt them knocking at the door of her throat, she felt them on the tip of her tongue. She was sure she was feeling love…yes it did feel like… love, it must be love. She wanted to say the words. She imagined his reaction to them, his unbridled happiness. He would insist they get dressed and get onto the hired Enfield (it had to be an Enfield) and loop through the roads of Goa to celebrate. 'Let's go eat breakfast at a shack and then get married. Right now,' he'd say and, she would laugh and tell him not be silly.

A gust of sadness howled through her body as she orgasmed. She held onto him with a vice-like grip. Why couldn't she say the words, she thought? Others said them so easily. She breathed into his neck slowly.

'You okay?' Anant asked.

'Hmmm,' she replied. She turned and he spooned her.

She didn't understand why people said things they didn't mean, she thought, as she stared at the red numbers on the digital alarm clock on the side table. Like the tailor who told her he would have her clothes ready tomorrow, but meant three weeks later. Like her friend who always said 'I'll call you back babe,' but never did. Like her mother who had said she was fine when Matrika knocked on the bathroom door. Thirty minutes later they found her on the floor, dead, pills strewn next to her. Why did people say words they didn't mean? No, she wouldn't say the words, *I love you*, till she knew.

She had made a vow to her nineteen-year-old self the day she watched the orange, dancing flames engulf her mum on the wooden pyre. She would tell the truth, always.

It was difficult, at times. When Professor Raghunathan who was teaching the Romantic Poetry module at Uni had asked her whether she knew who had written '*Shalini Raghunathan may love Coleridge, but she can't fuck him. He's dead,*' on the blackboard in college, she didn't say, 'I don't know,' but 'Yes.' She told a potential boss that yes, she did in fact mind if he smoked, despite the risk of putting him off her. If she wanted to bunk work, she didn't call in sick but confessed that she really didn't feel like coming in and could she please, please take the day off? She gave her friend her exact, honest opinion about her fiancé when asked and found a way to reach the same friend's house as she said she would, even though a cow came running down the road in a temper and knocked her over on the way.

'Your integrity, your passion' said Anant, when she once asked him what he liked about her. Words were sacrosanct and Matrika wasn't going to say the words, *I love you* to Anant till she was sure, bloody sure, 100% sure that she knew she was telling the truth. The problem was, they had now spent two years together, without her coming close. Matrika gave herself a deadline – one month - to reach a conclusion.

She stared at the inky, frothing sea, lost in thought while sitting on the balcony attached to their hotel room, as Anant slept. A cool, gritty breeze danced around her, mussing her hair and making the goose bumps rise through her skin. She thought back to another cool night; the night, but for which, they would have never found enough in common to hook up. The night they discovered that their mothers had both committed suicide.

She was covering the story of a powerful minister's wife's suicide for the television channel she worked for and he was the assigned editor. Staring at the image of the body wrapped in a white sheet being carried out of the five-star hotel over and again on the screen, as he looked for the right edit point, chilled her already cold skin in the dark, freezing edit suite. She wrapped the black shawl with orange paisleys embroidered on it tighter around her as memories rushed up, pushing past the barricade in her head and she found herself teetering on the edge of howling. When he asked her if she was okay, it all came tumbling out.

'My mother committed suicide as well.'

'So did mine,' he said and she had looked at him shocked.

'People thought I was sad. I was furious,' she said clenching the ends of the shawl inside her fist, 'Were you angry?'

'Yes, I thought she mustn't have really loved me if she could do this,' he said, his voice as flat as his palms, resting on his jean-clad thighs.

'Exactly. What a selfish thing to do. What a selfish, selfish thing to do.'

They couldn't edit the story fast enough. Later, she had cried and cried. He told her he had never spoken of his mother with complete honesty before. To anyone. He told her of the violence, of gripping his father's swinging hand, of begging his mother to leave, but that she chose another way. She told him about the depression, the memories of that orange nightie in which her mother lay with the pills around her, the bathroom she couldn't walk into for months after.

They spoke all night. In the edit suite, in the empty cafeteria with chairs upturned on the tables, on the steps outside the office building flanked by potted plants on either side. Her words were unstoppable and tripped over each other in haste. It was one of those rare occasions that she did not speak slowly and precisely, as was her habit; also the only time that he ever spoke at such length.

As they watched the sunrise, sipping tea at the *dhaba*, the ramshackle tea stall near the office, they felt drained, but euphoric.

They began spending all their time together. He'd arrange it such that he would edit her stories and they'd go out afterwards. They never invited their friends from work to join them. It felt like they were inside a snow globe, bobbing in the middle of an ocean, surrounded by the slapping sound of rising and falling water. The water was grey, the kind of grey you see in a painting. Their shared secret swirled and twirled inside the glass, a white mist.

The office grapevine soon caught on. 'You two?' said Rajan, the cameraman. 'Yeah, why?' asked Anant. 'You're like an idli-daal makhni combo you know? Unexpected.'

Unexpected perhaps, but then tragedy is a strong glue. When Anant lay down on his bed, elbows out, palms under his skull and gazed at the slowly rotating blades of the fan, she knew he was imagining himself hanging from there. He was wondering how thick the rope would need to be. How would it feel to not be able to breathe? Who would discover him? Of course, she knew he wasn't really planning to die, but when your parent commits suicide, you examine the possibility theoretically from time to time. She knew it without him having to say it. It's exactly the kind of thoughts she had when she glanced at the blue plastic covered strip of Paracetamol tablets on her side table that she was taking for a fever. Her mother had hundred and fifty. Would seventy-five do the trick?

When Matrika'a mother died, people had come bearing sympathetic words for what was left of their family – her father and herself. 'It's tough, but you will get through it.' 'I'm so, so sorry' 'I don't know what to say, I can't even imagine what you two are going through,' they would say as they sat on the sofa in the living room. Their eyeballs would shift awkwardly from the painting of Ravan with nine heads to the undusted crystal vase on the table and then back their faces. Their eyes, though awash with pity were, just eyes. Anant's eyes were mirrors. They reflected back what she was feeling.

That painting was possibly the only one in the world of Ravan with nine heads. Her mother had painted it. When she realised there wasn't enough space, she just left his tenth head out. It was so like her. Free from rules. Her father had looked at it and asked her mother, 'But why didn't you work it out beforehand?' Her mother rolled her eyes, as she often did when her husband said something so measured. Matrika tended to be like her father – exact. But, in her mother's presence, she'd felt unfettered, giddy, like anything was possible. No one else had picked up on the nine heads. Except Anant. He spotted it right away and laughed in delight. It had seemed like a sign.

However, once they stopped talking about their mothers there wasn't so much to talk about. Instead, they spoke about the day, office politics and where to go eat – desultory subjects like those. And increasingly, they spoke about how different they were.

'You're such a planner,' he had said one day as he saw her make a long to-do list, spectacles on her face, slipper-clad feet planted on her desk.

'Yes I know you like the spontaneous life,' she'd mumbled.

'Of course, so much more fun,' said Anant and flicked her specs off her nose, dangling them high so she'd had to jump for them.

And, the less they had to talk about, the more she wondered whether she loved him.

On their return flight from Goa to Delhi, Matrika watched the pretty, heavily made-up air stewardess walk by on high heels, manoeuvring the trolley down the aisle.

'They make them look like tarts. Deliberately of course,' she said.

He answered with a monosyllable, his eyes closed, head against the seat.

'I mean have you noticed how airlines never hire older women or anyone who isn't stick thin?'

'Yeah. Terrible.'

Back in Delhi, she asked herself if she was sure she loved him when she couldn't have long, rambling conversations with him.

Anant's idea of a heart to heart conversation was usually three sentences. What can one talk about in three sentences, thought Matrika? The sexualisation of air stewardesses, the rise of religious fundamentalism in India, the idea of fatalism vs. self-determination – these were not conversations that could be had in three sentences. So, she didn't have them with him.

She asked herself if she really, really loved him when she felt a surge of jealousy rise up in her as she read an interview with an English author, who said that she and her husband would spend evenings reading Keats to each other in front of the fireplace. She looked up longingly from the newspaper with the interview in it, to her bookshelf. It was crammed with books; books with dog-ears, paragraphs lovingly highlighted and notes in the margins. What she would give for Anant to pick up one of those books and read to her all evening. The first time he had seen her collection, he had stood there staring at it, playing with his bike keys. Up they went in the air and then down towards his palm. The only book he read in the last five years was The Da Vinci Code, he had told her.

She asked herself if she loved him first thing in the morning, between sleep and wakefulness, when she imagined an earthquake jolting her awake. She pictured the ground shaking violently, the cupboard shifting dramatically, the lights crashing, calling out to her father, careening through the house, the telephone wires entangling her legs, the wall giving way. She asked herself, would she remember to worry about Anant in those moments?

In the days after Goa, everything became a test of love -a conversation, a reaction or even a thought.

They had gone to Rajan's wedding, the night it came to a head, three weeks after the surprise trip to Goa. A cool breeze blew through the night, signalling the coming of winter. The bridal couple were under the *mandap,* decorated with white, sweet-smelling jasmine flowers in the centre of lawns bedecked with twinkling lights. The wedding ceremony was at a close. Guests in their finery showered the just-married pair with rose petals. Smoke wafted up from the traditional fire around which the couple had earlier walked seven times as they took their vows. The pot-bellied priest told the groom that the last decision he had ever made was to get married amidst much laughter. Its tinkling sound mixed with the air.

A voice suddenly called out to the priest, 'Panditiji! Get us married as well!' Matrika turned sharply. It was Anant.

The priest, a jovial sort of fellow, played along, 'Why not? A priest's got to earn!'

'Arre panditji, double money for the short notice,' shouted Anant.

Someone in the crowd yelled out, 'Two weddings for the price of one!' There was more laughter. Even the groom joined in, 'If I can do it, so can you!' he urged Matrika.

People didn't just get married like that. There were venues to book, decorators to meet, menus to decide and people to invite. The presence of the couple's parents was required. Well at least her father's. Anant wasn't in touch with his. Everyone thought this was one big joke. Everyone except Matrika who knew it wasn't. It was an ultimatum.

'Matrika,' he said, 'Will you marry me and make me the happiest man alive?' The throng of wedding guests erupted cheering.

She looked at him, her ears ringing like a wedding drummer, the *dhol vala* gone berserk, and remembered how he had held her the night of her mother's death anniversary, only a few days before Goa. His arms had made the image of the orange nightie with lace bordering its sleeves fade till it became black and white. She knew now that if she said no, she would not have those arms around her when she next needed them. So, she said the only thing she could, 'No.'

He resigned the next day. He packed his things in a cardboard box and came to say goodbye.

'Just like that?' she asked and he shrugged his shoulders. 'I'm used to starting over,' he said. He had when he walked out of his father's house and moved to Delhi.

They went and sat at the tea stall. The same tea stall where they had spent hours sitting on plastic chairs and rickety wooden tables, warding off the flies. The serving boy bought them their usual: two cups of tea and Masala Maggi noodles. They knew it was the last day they would ever see each other.

'I'm sorry,' she said.

'Nothing to be sorry. You either love someone or you don't.'

When he turned to walk away, the unexpected happened. Or perhaps it was the expected; it's when you lose someone that you know exactly what they mean to you, like you never did before. Just like she knew, when she lost her mother.

Emotion overwhelmed Matrika. It suffused her veins, sparkled in her blood and dusted her skin with gold. She had her answer. She loved Anant. It wasn't the love of a woman for her soul mate, no. It was a different love. A love that lay in between the folds of a friendship. Why had she thought that there was only one type of love? It was like the painting of the Ravan with nine heads, she laughed - free from rules.

It was there. The love was definitely there. She repeated silently 'I love you. I love you. I love you,' cherishing the words, getting drunk on the feeling as his bike disappeared into traffic.

Three Singers
KAVITA A. JINDAL

'What's in a name?' you might ask.

When you're mixed race; a lot hinges on it.

Take Perry Krishna Buckle.

When we met him at the singing class he introduced himself as PK.

It was not until the third lesson, when we congregated in the pub, that he told my twin sister and I that PK stood for Perry Krishna. His mother was Indian, he said, and she was from Mathura. His middle name was in honour of Mathura, Lord Krishna's birthplace.

My twin Sonali half-shrieked, half-laughed. 'Perry Krishna is a very odd name. 'But cute, too,' she added.

Then she dug her elbow into me, and announced to him, 'We're quite similar, you know. My middle name is Candida.'

PK looked taken aback. He regarded us closely. He had olive skin, light brown hair, flecked with even lighter wisps and brown eyes. In London, he could be from anywhere, any land, any race. Sonali and I had tried to figure out his ethnic antecedents but we never guessed he might be a person with the middle name of Krishna. Of course, we had half-expected that most of the people signing up to classes to sing *thumri* would have some connection to the Indian sub-continent.

That's what you might expect, but in our class of ten, two of whom only showed up once, four are not Asian and they are the ones most deeply interested in all aspects of north Indian light classical music, knowing more about *raag* and the traditions than us. They seem to have studied the music rather than merely enjoyed it. We're here to learn the songs we like to listen to when we are cutting or sewing. We'd put PK in the category of serious hobbyists on a spiritual musical journey; people whom we assumed had no exposure to this kind of music in their home. We learnt to love ghazals and *thumri* because our Dad made us listen to his CDs when we were growing up and given us intense explanations of the singers and the songs.

Everyone in our singing class is pleasant but PK is the only one near our age. We think he's in his late twenties, max early thirties. Although we head to the pub as a group, generally Sonali and I sit closest to PK and chat with him.

That evening after the third lesson PK turned to me after Sonali had announced her middle name. 'What's your name, Himani?' he asked. 'Full name, I mean'.

'Himani Charlotte Joy Dalzel Sahni.'

'That's a mouthful. Is your family of Indian origin?' PK asked hesitantly.

Of course, he knew we were. Presumably he could easily guess from my first and last name. What he was asking was, 'Are you mixed race? Really?'

It was obvious he hadn't guessed. Because, again, in London, with our dark hair, dark eyes, our average height and our names, we were firmly South Asian in our appearance. The slight give-away of Sonali's features, different from my own, were detected in India but not here. In one way our Dad was a stereotypical British Asian statistic because he was an ENT consultant. In his early youth he'd had a moustache but that had gone when he'd decided to settle in London. Our Mum was English, from the Lakes. She had studied architecture but didn't practice it. She had brown hair and light blue eyes which neither of us had inherited.

We're non-identical twins. We've always adored each other. We did have the occasional quarrel and it was usually because Sonali, who was older by two whole minutes felt she could boss me about, disapproved of the clothes I wanted to wear, or the subjects I wanted to study, or the boys I wanted to hang out with.

We parted ways at university so we could be free of each other and the people who knew us as twins. We enjoyed that phase of striking out on our own but somehow on our twenty-seventh birthday we agreed that we were most comfortable with each other and that we should work together. Sonali had the design experience and I had the MBA. After a year of toying with the idea we finally set up our own small fashion business. We named our label 'Two Singers'.

We loved singing, although we weren't very good at it. I was better at holding a tune, but Sonali opened her mouth more when she sang, as she wasn't shy, and she sang loudly and lustily. When we signed up for the group sessions of learning semi-classical songs, there was an unsaid assumption that we might meet some like-minded men in a neutral but fun environment. It was too bad that we were both currently single and unattached. I reckoned that even if we didn't meet anyone interesting we'd have spent some evenings doing something we loved. The classes were my idea because I don't like my time to be wasted.

Well, we met PK, and hit it off from the first session, but there weren't two of him. Unless…

My response to PK's question was to say that yes, we were Indian, or part-Indian and part-English, or just English, whichever way he liked to cut it; knowing that he would understand like nobody else would. I asked if he had a twin. Or a brother…

'I'm an only child', he replied.

At home Sonali and I guess PK's shoe size and shirt size. We guess what his mother might look like, since he seems to have gone entirely on his father. There are not many traces of Indian-ness in him. We wonder if he feels the same connection to our city, and whether he feels that pull towards Indian culture just because one parent took the time to inculcate an interest. We wonder what's brought him to the singing sessions.

I like him. He has an earnest air about him; he's not an aggressive type, his manners are refined, he's handsome.

He's a good listener but he doesn't tell us that much about himself, except when you ask him a leading question. Sonali, on the other hand, drip-feeds him too much information about us, including telling him I'm the 'geeky' one. He looked startled at that, rightly so. I suspect Sonali likes him too, more than she's letting on.

There's a one week break in our lessons and then we're back in the church hall for our first session after two weeks. We have six more to go. Then we can sign up to another term if we like. Our teacher is trying to gauge interest, as she has to fix the dates with the hall and pay a deposit. I wonder if our voices carry out into the nave of the empty church and if the statues turn their ears towards us. What would the Virgin Mary make of the songs we like to rehearse? *Thumri* lyrics and melodies were written for courtesans, about two hundred years ago, and sung by them to entice and entertain their patrons. The compositions were based on classical *raags* and on devotional folk lyrics, but the words are flirtatious, and about the relationship between lovers. Often we sing about an ache for a missing lover. I can relate to that, I think. It's not that I'm missing anyone in particular, at this moment, it's more that I'm missing having someone to miss. The songs make me weepy inside and I sing them softly.

I don't know what music sounded like when Jesus was a youth. All the hymn compositions came much later. But no doubt people all over the world sang or chanted and even two thousand years ago enthusiastic groups must have exercised their lungs together, and that joy hasn't changed.

Sonali pipes up to tell the tutor that we would sign up for the next term. 'We *love* it', she states. 'The classes have definitely met our expectations.'

I wonder if PK will last six more weeks in the course, and then another twelve thereafter. He's certainly been committed to the sessions, but life outside of this may take over. He's often mentioned his past travels. How many Thursday evenings will he give up to this amateur singing group? We are only six regulars now, with two others dropping in when they can. But the six of us, led by our teacher, make a good harmony.

We begin to sing a slow *thumri*. The lyrics of this one are based on Radha's love for Lord Krishna. '*Mora Sanyan Mose Bole Na*'. I sort-of join in, but as Sonali can be heard 'aaa – aaa - aahing' in a heartfelt but showy manner, I burn with indignation. She has a habit of flirting with the men I like before I can get round to it. Is she now going to make moves on PK without checking with me first?

In the event it is Sonali who is miffed when PK asks me to have a coffee with him.

'How about Saturday afternoon?' he said to me. 'I'm interested in hearing more about your fashion start-up.'
Sonali had gone to the loo when he asked. I broke it to her on the way home.

She was so astonished she actually said out loud what she was thinking. 'I thought he'd prefer me!'

That is what she said. My twin.

She sets my teeth on edge the way she assumes that every male in the universe will think of her as the more attractive one. We both know that it's not true; experience has proven that some men do exist who fancy me more than her. To be sure, in most of our unspoken wranglings over the same boys when we were teenagers, Sonali always felt she had first dibs. But why now, why today, does she believe PK would favour her?

What's so special? Is she preening herself on our differences? Sonali is precisely one inch taller than me. She makes a deal about it. Like she does about her pointy chin, which is like our mother's. She also has our mother's soft eyebrows, small nose and thin mouth. I have more striking brows and fuller lips.

My belly jabs at itself with fingers of acid. PK has individual looks I think, and an independent brain, and he asked me to coffee.

I won't let her upset me. She does say this sort of thing sometimes, oblivious to how it hurts me. I know we are all navigating the world based on our appearance and other people's gut response to it, but it is crazy that my sister can have the perception of only her own beauty.

'My personality,' Sonali says sharply, suddenly aware of what is going on in my head. 'I thought he would like my style.' She presses her lips into a pained expression, turning herself into the aggrieved party.

To appease her I say that PK wanted to hear more about our work and see our designs.

She snaps at me immediately: 'I'm the designer. Did you tell him that? *I* do all the work.'

I glare at her then. 'I'll be sure to tell him on Saturday,' I say. 'I'll tell him that you do all the work. I'll tell him I have the brain. I'll tell him I wrote the business plan. And I can cut and sew too. *And* I have to make the sales pitches with you.'

On Saturday, Sonali went for a swim while I met PK. I wasn't really sure that I was on a date. Coffee is not really a date date, is it? PK and I have a happy and easy conversation. The fact that we have sung together, when neither of us are cut out to be singers, makes us very relaxed in each other's company. I'm surprised that he actually does ask a lot of questions about our work.

'Was it really your business plan that got you the loan, Himani?' he says. 'I'd like to see it.' He notices my hesitation. 'If you don't mind, of course. You may not want a stranger checking your plan and stealing your secrets. But I may be able to offer some tips.'

'You're not a stranger,' I tell him, feeling flattered that he wants to see the schedule of business growth that I've devised. He told us before that he's an IT consultant but today he's shared the fact that he also has a business background. His father owns a small chain of supermarkets, a franchise of high-end watch dealerships, and real estate, among other things. PK says he usually doesn't like to mention his family business empire.

I am curious about why he's at the *thumri* class but I don't ask him outright.

I babble a bit about my reasons instead. 'Some friends like to learn Bollywood dancing. I mean, not just Asian friends, but everyone. But when it comes to loving Hindi film songs, both old and new, it's only Indians, Pakistanis, and Bangladeshis, right? Some of our friends think it's weird that we're more interested in light classical music. I keep telling them that often the film songs are based on classical raags. They don't get our obsession with *thumri* but I think it's something that reminds us of our childhood. Then, we used to sigh that we were being force-fed this additional culture; now we listen to it by choice, especially when we're working.'

PK gives an understanding nod. He discovered *thumri* when he was dragged to concerts in Delhi while he was visiting friends. He had such a wonderful time on that visit that he was trying to re-create some of that magic in London. 'I'm trying to gain more of an insight into the artform so I can fully appreciate it when I go to a live recital again,' he says, looking endearingly earnest.

I let my heart indulge in little leaps of delight. I want to sit closer to him, touch his hands. I could tell him about upcoming concerts at the South Bank and we could go together.

'I don't even fully understand the words,' he says wistfully. 'At least Sonali and you speak the language.'

'Not very well,' I assure him. 'But yes, of course, we can get by. As for the lyrics, they are not that different from song to song. My mother always says: there's the monsoon, and the lovers are either separated and pining, or about to get together. Even she's an expert.'

I don't mention that he sometimes mispronounces the words we sing in the class.

I'm staring at his shoulders, thinking I could have a fusion Indo-Western jacket made for him and how good he would look in it, when he asks, "Coffee again, Himani?' Next Saturday? Same time, same place?'

Another coffee? I think. Another Saturday afternoon? A tame time, I think.

I try not to be too disappointed that he pecks me airily on both cheeks when he goes off. I mean I *am* disappointed but he hasn't led me to expect anything more.

At the Thursday singing lesson Sonali is subdued and I'm grateful for that. She's not muscling in now. He's attracted to me, I think to myself. Me. He likes me for my intellect and poise and self-sufficiency, and my wavy thick hair, all things he's complimented me on. I find myself smiling a lot more at everyone in the class. When I exchange a look with PK I know I shine with happiness.

The next Saturday PK tells me more about himself. He seems quite intent that I get to know his background. He seems to have been lonely at boarding school while being a high-achiever. He doesn't say so, but I'm drawing my own conclusions as he shares some of his memories. His parents are divorced. He asks me my experience of being mixed race. 'Do you feel English? British? Indian? Wholly of one culture? A bit of both? Disconnected from both?'

'Disconnected?' I say, puzzled. 'I think of myself as multifaceted, blessed. I am not A *or* B; I am A+B, I am lucky to draw the best from two cultures.'

I am very emphatic on this point and he quickly nods, although he looks sad.

'You couldn't possibly have a problem, PK, with not fitting in,' I say, 'not with your looks.'

He grins then. 'I don't have a problem; I'm just sometimes confused. Now, has the intelligent multifaceted person brought the business plan?'

I love his cheekbones when he grins like that. I hand him a folder of some pages that I'd photocopied for him. I did want to show off – I couldn't help it.

'If you don't mind, I'll read it right now,' he says. He orders another coffee and studies the document. I begin to wonder then if one reason he prefers my company is that I'm quiet, unlike Sonali. I'm watching his concentration but not showing how restive I'm getting. What kind of relationship does he want? The question races around my brain while I try to tranquilise my disobedient heart.

PK finishes reading and returns the folder to me. 'Do you need an investor, Himani?' he asks.

'Why?' is the first response that escapes my lips.

'If you do, I would like to invest in your business.'

My insides sink and soar at the same time. A cash injection would be marvellous. PK, essentially an outsider, showing conviction in our work is even more wonderful. But if he becomes our business partner will he be a boyfriend? Wouldn't that be too complicated? Focus on the positive, I think. We could employ a tailor. We must have won PK's trust if he wants to put money into our venture. He must be sure he'll get a good return. He must be *very* impressed with my business plan.

PK leans forward. 'I feel like you're my sisters.'

I want to crash through the floor. Yet I'm still sitting here, hiding my wounds. I am beginning to comprehend him. He's investing in *family*. We've won his affection. But I haven't managed to steal his heart and fly away with it and I won't be bringing it back with the monsoon clouds.

I haven't managed to say a word to him yet. PK raises his coffee mug to his lips, twists his mouth in distaste at the dregs, puts the mug down and smiles. 'Himani Charlotte,' he croons softly, persuasively, lifting a finger. 'Sonali Candida'. Another finger. 'Perry Krishna'. He lifts a third finger. 'A minor re-brand is all that's required,' he says.

'Three Singers'.

To London
MONA DASH

I was in London after fifteen years. Fifteen years since London and love had happened to me.

Just an hour ago we had checked into the Savoy; Niren was already in the bar, busy with yet another meeting. He was always busy, he enjoyed working hard so that we could relax and enjoy the time he didn't have. He was such a gentleman.

'You don't have to work,' he'd told me when we got married. 'I make enough money for both of us. For as many of us as we want to become.'

I subsumed into becoming the four of us. A son and daughter arrived within a few years. We didn't have to wait too long or try too hard. None of the disasters which sometimes affected other couples. My Facebook had happy pictures of us; in exotic locales; Dubai, Florida, Barbados, in our bungalow in Delhi; Sarika and Sanjay performing in school plays, winning trophies in sports.

And here we were in our plush family suite, the window overlooking the Strand. It looked the same. A lifeline through the city bordered by the Somerset House, Adelphi theatre, Coutts bank, Smollensky bar; names I had never really forgotten, sights I had never really stopped seeing. I could hear the children arguing.

'Snape says Sectum sempra, not sectumsempura, all in a rush.' Sanjay was saying.

'And that's ex-actly what I said.' Sarika retorted.

I stood still looking out at the warm London evening. My view, my memories, my London.

#

It is year 1999, and I am walking briskly along the Strand, talking on my phone. I have got out of the Holborn tube, and walked past India House, the Lyceum theatre showing Lion King, the Savoy. He is running late and will reach only after 5 p.m. I have some time to spare, so I walk into Topshop. London's fashion entices me; it is hard to walk by shops without stepping in. A black skirt on sale. Slits on the side. Nice and tight. Reduced from £25 to £10, and in my size! A bargain.

Then cross across to Trafalgar square. On hot summer days, the fountains are on, kids paddle in the shallow water around it. In the square, I have seen lighted Christmas trees, Diwali celebrations, and one Sunday, even 'Rath Yatra', the chariot festival of Lord Jagannath. The city never fails to surprise.

The square, fittingly, is perfect for our rendezvous. There are several benches set in a circle, hidden from the main road. It is always full of tourists, but their attention is taken by Nelson, the lions, the plinths or the pigeons. Not by us, the couple in a corner trying to hide from everyone's eyes. Even now in the dusk, there are people taking pictures before the weak sun disappears, plunging London into another October evening.

I notice a girl posing against the lion and a man taking her picture.

'Do you want me to take one of you?' I ask. They nod. They stand arm in arm, the girl arranges her fringe so that it falls over her forehead, and the man holds her tighter.

'Can you take one more, please?' he asks. This time they turn towards each other, their lips meet. I take a couple more shots. They thank me as if I have performed a huge deed of kindness.

He never agrees to take pictures with me, even though I promise to be careful. But he is terrified, almost as if the picture will acquire its own voice and shout and scream about us to anyone he knows.

I find an empty bench and sit down and wait. And wait. He is usually late. My knight in shining armour, my knight who unfortunately is not mine.

I see him before he notices me. That familiar, slightly lopsided gait, walking so fast that the pigeons fly out in alarm. He is tall, but not so tall as to look ungainly, sturdy but not butch. In my eyes, he is perfect. Greenish brown eyes and floppy hair. Twenty-nine, in love and in London. It can't get better than this, except that the object of my love, this handsome man now sitting next to me, now lifting my face to kiss me as if there is no tomorrow, is married.

In his defence he has never hid this. Nor the fact that he loves his children, smiling at him from his wallet. Two golden haired kids, a boy and a girl. I haven't seen the wife's picture nor do I want to. It's easier for me, as I am free to imagine a pinched, thin-faced woman and not some blonde Venus.

'Look, I bought this skirt. While I was waiting for you,' I say.

'Let's see?'

I pull it out of the bag.

'I meant on you…why don't you wear it? Now?'

'Here, in the middle of the city?' I ask amused.

It is almost dark, maybe no one will notice. Even if they do, I don't really mind. Only once, we only live once, we tell each other often. A finite time granted to us to have our infinite pleasures. So I pull the skirt over my head and deftly slip out of my work trousers. Gracefully extricate the trousers from my high heels. I twirl before his admiring gaze. If anyone has caught me in their frame, they will probably just add me to London's idiosyncrasies.

'Amazing, so sexy!!' He is old fashioned that way. Skirts and sling back shoes always work for him.

He has only twenty minutes today. Then he will rush to Charing Cross for his train to Rickmansworth, or some such faraway suburb in zone 6 a. His wife is going to the movies, so he can't afford to be late. But I don't complain. Even twenty minutes is worth it, to feel alive. To let the heavens descend on our small and routine lives. For that's what I feel when with him. The gloriousness of passion! The freedom of letting go! Some long kisses later and his embarrassed smile at his obvious stiffness; (Everyone is looking at you, I tease) we say our goodbyes.

#

Sarika dashed into my reverie.

'I am hungry! Are we going out?'

She always was. I wished Sanjay would have some of her appetite. Two years younger, at nine, she was the same size as him. She took after Niren, and Sanjay after me, the wrong way round. A small imperfection in our otherwise perfect family picture.

'I don't want to eat yet,' Sanjay says.

'I want a pizza. Can I get a pizza?' Sarika says.

Her voice had taken on the little girl whine she knew I disliked. Pepperoni pizza, thick crust, melting cheese, busy restaurants; I wished instead I could stand here with my thoughts.

'Let's go downstairs and get something,' I give in.

#

We had visited most of Europe, America, Australia even but never London. I had managed to steer the interest away, citing issues of visas, weather and so on.

But the call of the city was too great. All of their friends had been to London, almost every new Bollywood movie was shot in London, and now there was the Harry Potter studio and the Harry Potter bus tour.

'Why aren't we going to LONDON?' Sanjay demanded. 'It's only Mom who lived there not us!'

'London, it is then!' Niren said. I realised he didn't remember my previous refusals or maybe had never read much into it.

Somewhere in me, curiosity burned. How was my city in all these years? The city I'd loved, more than loved. The city I knew like the back of my hand, like the back of his hand. Leaving it was hard, but it had to be done, like death, in a way.

So here were we, in the summer holidays. Ten days in London.

'I used to shop here,' I said, when we went for a walk later that evening. Topshop was still here, ensconced between Bella Italia and Pizza Express. No one heard me though. We crossed the Strand, walked down Duncannon Street, the post office on the right, Trafalgar square looming before our eyes just like it did years ago. The pigeons have left, over the years they have become a nuisance, I have read. The children run towards the lions.

My bench is still here, I sit down on it.

'Rita, smile!' Niren calls out and takes a picture of me, smiling beyond him into the past. My special past. Just one of the many places in this city where we'd met and kissed as if there was no tomorrow. And there was no tomorrow for us. He'd known that. I had to learn over the years. I had to learn to let go of love and still live.

#

I spend evenings going to the theatre, the opera, the Royal Albert hall; sometimes he comes, if he can. Otherwise I go alone, holding on to the memory of his kisses, his lips on me at lunchtime on a park bench. He comes to London on work a few days in the week. We try to meet when we can. He tries his best. I still believe someday I will have more.

'I can't leave them, my children. I can't break their home,' he says.

When he said he hardly slept with his wife anymore, I believed it. When he said I was the woman he really wanted, I believed it. I just never understood why he couldn't leave her. It was only after my children that I did. When I held Sanjay and Sarika in my arms, I knew that they were all that mattered. I could never desert them, not for the wildest love in the world. Perhaps he felt the same with the golden haired boy and girl.

'You are the only one who wants me for being me. My family loves my role, as a husband, as a father. Not the real me,' he whispers to me. Everybody deserves such a love in their lives, he says. Everyone needs such a love to stay alive, I agree. The time in bed, the time out of bed; it's enough to dazzle my day.

One of the inconveniences is the flatmate. I can only afford a shared flat, so we can't meet in mine. Which is why we must meet in London's many corners, or hotels. Once, my flatmate is away and he manages to get away from home. I wear my peacock blue saree and make him an Indian meal.

#

The next day, when our cab goes past Paddington station, I see it is still there. The innocuous looking Westpoint hotel, opposite the Garfunkel, thirty steps from the underground. Mute witness to stolen mornings, long afternoons.

The basic lounge with its grey carpet, the narrow steps up to our usual room. The quick nod the man at reception gives me. He strikes the deal. Sometimes £40 for half a day. Sometimes £25 for two hours. If they have no rooms, then further up the road there is the Crocus. Slightly more expensive, we have to pay up to £50. Usually he pays. Once he suggests I pitch in so that we can afford something better.

But in my world the man pays. Especially if he is married, is older and doesn't have the guts to leave a marriage for love. I only tell him this when I leave London. I spit the words out on his face.

#

I had first come to London, in 1996, to attend a conference. The event was in the Savoy, but my stay had been arranged in a bed and breakfast in South Kensington. I still remembered my first tube journey, the feel of that morning.

I walk out into a cold, somewhat grey morning. A park on my right, a flower stall just outside the station and I catch a whiff of a light fragrance. Roses, tall lilies, what an abundance of colour! Do people buy so many bouquets on a daily basis? In India I live a car to office to house existence.

None of this walking on tubes and escalators; I struggle on my stilettos. There is a slight drizzle. I have a thick coat and a long scarf but I am not accustomed to the chill of the wind. Everyone is walking fast as if pulled along together on some unseen elastic band. If I ever come to London again, I will practice before – high heels, a fast pace, hot coffee mugs, walk straight, looking ahead as if a distant horizon is getting closer. The smells of the early morning coffee, the crispness of the cold air, something I don't get much in Mumbai where I live – Maybe that's the moment I fall in love with London.

Finally I reach the hotel; Notting Hill, Hugh Grant walking in to meet Julia Roberts with his blockbuster card, the same chandelier hanging above my head.

I am late, and it's never nice to enter a conference room, when the presentation has begun and the room is deathly quiet. The door squeaks and all eyes turn to me. I look around for an empty seat, and notice someone gesturing. It's in the middle row, and he moves his legs to let me go past, into the seat next to him. I say a grateful thank you and settle in. It's towards the end of the talk, that I notice the man's badge. Matt Johnson. Head of Marketing. The Interactive agency. I almost shout out, I have heard of him. He is a prolific speaker and very respected in the industry. I pass him my card – Rita Mehta, Director, Agency Meritas. Impressive, he writes on his notepad. His mouth creases into a smile.

We chat in the coffee break. They are very interested in India, he says. Like most organisations are, so I am not surprised. People throng around him and he introduces me to everyone. I have never collected as many business cards. I dream of acquiring several new clients in London and moving to manage the office.

'Come on, let's escape,' he says when the networking drinks is over. I have already drunk a few glasses of wine. A bit light headed, a bit jet lagged, but on a high. A glittering city, a charming man. He suggests dinner and we walk towards Piccadilly, then turn into other small street. Peak Street, I read.

'There we are, Osterizia,' he says. It's a small Italian restaurant. 'One of my favourites.' I want to remember everything about this evening.

'You know a city from its rivers,' he says, when I say I want to see more of the city. We go for a walk along the river after dinner. I try to remember Wordsworth's 'Upon Westminster Bridge' from my school days, but he says they weren't taught the poem.

We escape; not that time, not the time we meet in Mumbai some months after when he visits, but a year later, on my next trip to London; into a fairy tale world where there is only sensation. Passion. No commitments, no promises to break the flow. Time spent in whispers and touches. He often describes the moment he saw me at the door of the conference room; framed in beauty, looking just a little unsure. He had beckoned, hoping I would come and sit next to him. He talks of a strong connection he felt, he admires my drive and energy. He compliments often.

Then my company posts me to London. And our story begins. This is love. Such a powerful searing love which governs my day. And his. He calls me the minute he leaves home. We meet over lunch breaks and business trips. He has his reputation and family to protect. I have nothing to lose and London is the willing accomplice to my love. We sit on benches in Green Park; lie on the grass near the rose garden in Hyde Park, watch the runners go by in Regents Park, kiss in dark corners of the pub opposite great Portland Street; every corner of London has a special moment, a special place in my body.

#

For all his fears and caution, his wife finds us out. He has forgotten to delete a text from me. 'Same time tomorrow? Can't wait, love you!' I have written. No name and my number is not saved in his address book. She calls me, and when I answer 'Rita Mehta' she hangs up. Some more times, over and over again. She confronts him, he explains me away; I am a professional colleague from India, much younger, he is like my mentor. I had meant to write 'with love', and not 'love you', but I often do silly things like that. He calls me from the living room, and coaches me with this story. I am to downplay all the love, all the moments we have devoured. Unfortunately for him, she has been clever enough to place a recorder in the room. Now she knows everything. She calls me again, in a whisper – 'You bitch. I am getting him to take an Aids test. You and your den of iniquity. It is humiliating,' she adds, 'to think he had to go after something foreign.'

I don't hear from him for a few lonely days; then he calls, from a phone booth, where he can't be traced. She watches his every move. Ugly words have come up; divorce, settlements, custody. I console him. I wonder if he is relieved that it has all come out in the open. That he will be free to leave her, to love now. But, the mastermind that he is, he manages to keep her by his side. He promises me off; promises he will never meet me again. But he explains he doesn't intend to keep his promise. 'There is no reason to stop our beautiful love. We just have to be more careful, I will get a different number to call you from, I can't meet you as frequently, as she might have me followed, you see…but I will definitely meet you. I can't forget you…'

But what about me? I finally see that all he would ever offer was the leftover of his days.

Destiny has its own timing. My mother calls the same week, when I am adrift, and mentions a marriage proposal. An established family, a good boy, hardworking, and wealthy. Without further questions I agree. 'Err maybe you should see him?' my mother asks. Like a dutiful daughter, I answer I respect their choice. They are relieved. I make plans to go back for the engagement.

It is then that I meet Niren. From a distance, it is all fine, it's only at close quarters, that you notice the vitiligo on his face. Around the eyes, the mouth, later I would see white islands on his back. I see the worry in my parents' eyes. But I don't back out; it doesn't seem to be reason enough to refuse someone, when the most obvious one, Love, wasn't even being discussed. We get engaged, we get married, a dazzling Indian wedding. I need the finery to forget the touch of love that had kept me in its hold for three years.

All in the matter of a few weeks. Nice, practical. Nothing as painstaking as love. Life followed effortlessly after that.

Niren had asked me about past loves. I told him about my college sweetheart, and that was it. Wasn't there anyone in London? I was too busy working, I said. But I know I have ignored others; the smile of the charming French man, the funny English guy I met in the local pub. For me it was about secrets, pleasure, his voice, his smiles, and his touch like no other.

#

I have been thinking of him, of the past, myself, all the six days we have been here. I see people filing out of the conference room we had sat in years ago. Suddenly under the same chandelier of the Savoy where we stood and chatted so many years ago, I feel like calling him. Just once. To hear the past again. I still remember his number; you can't forget a number you dialled or heard from at least ten times a day even after fifteen years. You don't forget the number you had to stop yourself from dialling after I left London. Most people in England tried to hold on the same mobile number, so it was worth a try. I call from the little prepaid phone Niren had given each of us.

'Matt Johnson,' the same lilt in the voice. Just like before. Fifteen years melt away. I hang up.

He calls back in a minute. 'Sorry, I just had a call from this number?'

'It's me,' I say.

For a moment there is silence. Then much softly, 'Rita is that really you?'

'Just passing by, with my family. Thought would say hello,' I say brightly.

'Can I see you?'

He lives in St Alban's now. He's retired, so he's hardly ever in London. Could I go over?

I couldn't meet him anymore. I needed to meet him, just once. I was not the same girl anymore. The passionate girl lived somewhere within. I was Mrs Soni with her two children. I was Rita Mehta without a care in the world.

Niren emerges with Sarika and Sanjay. They had been at the concierge asking about some day trips out of London.

'I need to check my diary and let you know. Will call later, alright?' I say, hanging up.

'Who was that?'

'Just a friend. Was wondering if we could meet, but they are so far out, not sure if it's worth it. St Albans.'

'Maybe we could all go there? The children can see a little more of England. St Albans is quite nice, isn't it?'

That was my man, my husband, always wanting to find a solution for everything. With him you didn't have to think or worry. Sometimes you even struggled to feel anything, as he had sorted it before you felt it. Was it the imperfections on his skin that made him want to perfect things, not realising he couldn't always control everything?

'I don't want to go there,' Sanjay says immediately.

'No one is going anywhere,' my voice sounds unusually sharp.

'Maybe she could come over, and I can take the kids out somewhere?' Niren suggests.

'Legoland.' Sarika says.

'Lord's,' Sanjay says.

'Done,' Niren says.

The plan comes through. I call again and when I ask if he can come, he says that's what he wanted to propose. His wife is away at the county fair. He won't have too long unfortunately, but perhaps we could have lunch.

Niren and the kids go to Legoland, with one of his associates and their kids.

'Can I buy 'Stephanie's beach house?' Sarika says.

'Lego shouldn't have been made for girls! Can I buy the Death Star?'

They leave. I imagine them squabbling over the rides, I wonder how their day will go and whether they will be fine. Niren says I needn't worry.

#

All afternoon I walk by myself, diving into streets I know and those I don't quite remember. The city seeps into me. A promise, a hope that the future could be as sweet as the past. For our love remained; our passion was still here in London. It shone and glittered in the city's hidden corners. It rose in the fireworks over the Thames every New Year eve. It lived in London's wine bars and restaurants, a fleeting whisper amidst all the noise. Every time two strangers met, smiled, and claimed the city, our love was rejuvenated. People could be forgotten, but not love, not London.

He is outside as I walk up to Charing Cross station. Not late for a change. He is heavier, certainly. And so am I. No more that skinny, agile, corporate girl who got in and out of clothes at somebody else's behest. Grown from my London size eight to my current size twelve.

We shake hands. If I saw him now, I would have overlooked him like yet another middle aged English man. I start talking, rambling, tell him about Sarika and Sanjay.

'How are your children?' I ask.

'Hardly children anymore! Lucas has moved out with his girlfriend. Lilly is going to university.' They had names, the golden haired children. 'And you! Two kids! You look the same though…just a little,' he thinks, 'wiser…elegant!'

'I look substantial,' I laugh. I notice some wrinkles on his hands. I have worn my sapphire, diamond ear studs and pendant – Niren showered me with expensive jewellery every birthday. I have dressed with care, fitting dark blue trousers and a cream blouse, a shawl across my shoulders. I look so much older, I know.

It is easy to talk to him. He was after all my best friend; he could always make me laugh. He does a lot of gardening these days.

'Fuchsias and tomatoes,' he laughs.

I haven't worked since the kids, I tell him.

'But you were so good! Do you not miss it?!' he exclaims, as if something precious is lost. I did initially, but my life is full. Socially, culturally, I defend. His wife isn't keeping too well. But she still hasn't forgotten, she keeps a check on him. Somewhere in his eyes, in his smile, I see the past. That past which I had turned my back on, but in doing so, had I actually preserved it perfectly? We go to Zizzi's for lunch. It would be so easy, I think. We could go back to the Savoy, to the empty suite. I look at his hands; the familiar gold ring, the nails cut clean. Would they feel the same, anymore?

The past fifteen years have gone by at a steady pace. In order to place a memory, I had to look for milestones, a birthday, an end of term day. But those years in London were vivid, the moments and memories lived without any references, without any anchors to tie them down. Should life be measured in intensity or time?

Over the years I often thought of my love. It sustained me, through the routine. It was because I had known love's glittering body that I could live the rest of my life without its temptation.

We have finished our spaghetti Bolognese and prawn linguine. A glass of wine each. It's time to pay the bill, and I insist I pay. He gives in. He asks about my plans for the rest of the day. I will figure something out, I say.

Outside, he bends down to kiss me, our lips graze. Ever so slightly.

'Thanks for your time. It meant a lot,' he shrugs his shoulders. 'I have missed you.'

'Thanks for making the time,' I say formally. I am not able to say anything more. I reach out, touch his face for an instant.

If he knows me, he will understand.

Naz
IMAN QURESHI

You know those big dogs on the street? The ones with chunky studded collars and massive jaws. Look as if they could rip you apart like a chicken wing? I always loved them. Mum used to hold her breath and cross the road if she ever saw one. It was only years later I learnt that back when she was little, she'd been attacked by a dog. Since then, she was afraid of going near them. I guess that made it even stranger how she kept going back to my dad. I never got it. But those dogs. With their big smiley faces, broad shoulders and sad eyes. That was all I needed in life.

The third time she went back to him I moved out. Pip pip cheerio to my offer to read Biological Sciences at Oxford University, and good riddance to the Merlot swilling future he had carefully plotted out for me from before I was born. I decided that I would be his shame.

I rented a little one bed on Leith Walk, made a visit to the Cats and Dogs home and brought back the biggest butchest Staffordshire bull terrier I could find. She was a cuddly giant really, but looked so tough even big men would walk a wee semicircle round her in the street. Doris, she was called. I didn't name her. I remembered Mum saying how her parents had tried to change her name when they emigrated to Scotland from Pakistan, and how she cried so much they had to change it back. So Doris she remained.

I got a job chopping onions at the curry place downstairs, and drank beer at a pub on Lothian Road. Doris would lie beside my stool, thumping her tail happily on the wooden floor when someone was brave enough to pet her head. I brought home the odd boy from time to time. Thick as bricks if you ask me, but it was easy. No frills, no fuss, no fancies. Bish Bosh. Job done. They never called, I never complained. The next morning Doris and I would head down to Leith with a sandwich bag of sausages for us to share and watch the addicts prop themselves up in doorways begging for a few quid for their next hit. I'd drop some money into their cup sometimes, mostly out of guilt. Mum was an addict of sorts too, after all. Trapped in her old habits.

She would call sometimes, but I always hung up before she got too upset. Dad stopped ringing after I threatened to call the police. The irony of having a private school educated Pakistani daughter working at a Pakistani takeaway was just about enough for his white liberal sensibilities to bear. He wasn't going to risk having the police nosing around his other dirty laundry and wrecking his lah-di-dah architect reputation, so he did the clever thing and let well enough alone. So it was just me and Doris. Life wasn't half bad.

Then *she* came along and turned everything upside down. Bouncing out into the car park with a ponytail and a yoga mat slung across her shoulder like some Californian yuppie. And before I could stop her, Doris was bounding up to this complete stranger, circling her ankles like the Tasmanian

Devil. Next thing I know she was bending down and rubbing Doris' jowly cheeks, and letting herself be licked across the face like a scene right out of Lassie. And just as I tried to apologise she started off:

'Oh, is she yours – she's absolutely lovely. I had one just like her. They're so misunderstood aren't they? Such gentle things really.' And of course, any friend of Doris' is a friend of mine. So when she suggested dinner at some vegan diner full of hipster tree huggers in knit sweaters, I didn't even think to protest.

The food was vile; how many variations of bean can you get? Soy and tofu and curd. All that extra methane can't be very environmentally friendly. And this girl – 'Katrina, Katrina Harte, but you can call me Kat' - was exactly the opposite of me: bubbly and chatty and full of faith in the goodness of humanity or some such nonsense.

So imagine my surprise when I went from rolling my eyes and picking at an overpriced bean burger in some trendy diner to waking up under a patchwork quilt on her couch, with Kat tucked up on the other end, and Doris snoring beside us on the rug. It was so lame, that for a second I thought I'd been transported to some cheesy Hollywood rom-com from the 90s. And then:

'Good morning, hope you slept all right on the sofa. Let me make you breakfast.' And breakfast wasn't just tea and toast. No. Pancakes, strawberries, syrup. Had I spent the night with Delia Smith's granddaughter? But forget who she was, who was I?

'Oh yes, lovely, thank you, yes I'd love some tea – Earl Grey would be grand, thanks.' I don't even like Earl Grey! And she gave it to me in this wee porcelain teacup with a little slice of lemon on the side. And then we talked more. I didn't even know there were that many conversations you could actually have. Turns out I was wrong. Eventually around lunchtime, off I finally went with my day. But she wanted to see me again, and again, and again. More talking and more talking. And it was – nice. Really nice.

Anyway, for like the tenth time, we arranged to meet up after work. I was only working a lunchtime shift at the restaurant so I went home first to shower. But something was up, because I'd bitten my nails right down to the skin and changed my clothes about twelve times. Finally, I resigned myself to the fact that I am just not a creative person when it comes to fashion and the like, settled for my usual jeans and hoodie combo, and off I went. Doris on a lead and me, practically dancing along to the Top 40 on my headphones. The Top 40. Me! Imagine that.

I was a little early so I waited. The sun was low in the sky over New Town, and Edinburgh was all warm and hazy in the light. Eventually she appeared and all I could make out was this shadow against the sun walking towards me, carrying a picnic basket like a park ranger. I mean who did she think I was? Yogi bear?

'Right, this is ridiculous', I thought. There I was with Beyonce blaring in my ears, talking about a sunset, about to go up Calton Hill. With a picnic. But I was there now, and so was she. So up we went, to the top of the hill, but not quite to the very top, because it was rammed with Chinese tourists wearing Oxford University hoodies, I mean were they lost or something? We went the other way, round past those columns to a little bench that was tucked away. And we were talking – still talking, always talking, I had no idea what we said to each other anymore, but it was just so easy.

We sat down and Ranger Kat unpacked her picnic basket – there was red wine, cheese, bread, beef bresaola because except for sausages, I don't eat pork, and of course treats for Doris. I mean she even brought little plastic cups for the wine. What she did forget was a knife. So I pulled out my Swiss Army penknife, which I carry everywhere in case of an emergency, and she gave me a funny look, then laughed.

I smiled back awkwardly but really, I couldn't quite understand why she even bothered with me. I mean, I took a look at myself in the mirror during all my costume changes, and well - I'm a little tubby, quite awkward. I've got Mum's Pakistani sideburns and my dad's pasty Scottish skin. And really, it's like Kat and I have stepped out of that stupid kids nursery rhyme - I'm snakes and snails and she's all lavender, spice and everything nice.

And we sat there talking and cutting off bits of cheese with my penknife, and sipping wine, and the sun was setting, and it was oddly cold up there, so we sat quite close together, shivering a little, and talking, still talking, until finally she looked at me and asked,

'What are we doing?'

And suddenly I got all awkward and didn't know what to say. I mean, what were we doing? I took a big, long, slow glug of my wine to buy myself some thinking time. And I was watching her, watching her face, her gentle eyes. And the light was just right, her brown hair all ginger in the sun, her eyebrows creased up in a frown, maybe because she was anxious, or maybe just from the glare, and her little red lips were pursed, tense.

And I just didn't know what to say. How could I tell her that I was a disaster and not worth it, and we'd only end up wrecking each other's lives and being miserable and hating each other, when all I wanted to do right then was lean in and kiss those cold nervous lips of hers? And when, instead I just sat there useless, not saying anything she just went right ahead and did it anyway. Leant in and kissed me.

Five months and eight days later here I am – not that anyone's counting. I just happen to have a good memory. But the thing is, it's been that long and I'm not even sick of her. Surely after all that time, all that talking, I'd be bored. But I'm not. It's like the opposite of bored. And sometimes, when I look at her sleeping beside me, her lovely soft hair fanned out on the pillow like some Disney princess, and I feel my stomach flutter in a way that's never happened before, I remember exactly why she's trouble.

That feeling. It just creeps up on you like some ninja in the night, doesn't it? Or like getting drunk for the first time. Like before you know it it's too late and you've got your head in a toilet bowl retching your guts out and wishing someone had warned you before you drank that twentieth alcopop. Maybe I shouldn't be so hard on Mum, if this tummy fluttery thing is what makes her go back to him.

I wonder if he was nice to her back in the day. If, when they first met, they talked for hours and hours. About family. And life. And hopes and dreams, like he was Barack Obama. And I wonder if she was there, just like me, lapping it up like some stupid puppy, late into the night.

I remember her dressing up in these gorgeous saris and going to his posh events. And he'd pack away his temper, put on this smug smile and act like he was serenely proud to be seen with her. But even then I'd notice his firm hand dig into her back, and his eyes flicking back and forth from the nearest cocktail waitress. Oriental architecture was his thing, and an Oriental wife the perfect handbag for the reputation he had built for himself.

Mum tried to tell me sometimes about the good days. How he talked her parents round, how he made her laugh, how intelligent he was. How, in a world where she was a Paki, he made her feel like a Princess. But the next day I'd see the bruise on her arm, and the broken ashtray in the bin and wonder whether she thought it was a fair price to pay for a handful of good memories and a Birkin bag.

And it's not just my parents but my friends too. For all the beaters, there are ten cheaters. Roz with her boyfriend who slept with a prostitute. Danny whose girlfriend sexts other boys. Vix whose *boyfriend* sexts other boys. And then they run round calling it 'love'. There's nothing lovely about it.

It's for saps who watched too much Disney when they were little. But at least I'm not some Bambi-eyed dreamer looking for love in the seedy neon lit bars of Edinburgh's public triangle. Because come on, all anyone is really after is a diddle now and then, and you can pretty much do that yourself. And the love bit? Well I have Doris. I'll always have Doris. And that feeling I get when I look at Sleeping Beauty over here? Well, I know what that means.

Now, five months and eight days in, and Katrina Harte would like to meet the parents. Wonders where they are, why I never see them, suggests that they couldn't possibly be that bad – anyone who produced me, must have done something right.

It was our first fight. Five months of picnics, dog walks on the beach, and even a bloody yoga class - which wasn't actually as torturous as I expected - and now this. It had clearly been building up, bothering her for a while. Sometimes she would go quiet, then sigh and say something about how she wished I'd open up. If she only knew how far I'd come already.

So last night, as she vented and then later cried about how she felt like I was shutting her out, holding back, and maybe I didn't really want to be with her at all, all I could do was sit there, as dumb as Doris. What excuse could I possibly give? How could I tell her about my mother, and the father she'd chosen for me? The bruises and the shouting and the tears? Where would I start? How could Katrina Harte's beautiful brain full of flowers and fairytales ever

76

understand? How would she have looked at me, treated me, if she knew? What if she thought it was my fault? That I was a bad daughter. That I'm still a bad daughter, and we couldn't play happy families anymore.

So that's how we went to bed. Kat, in tears and me just wanting to make it all better, but knowing I couldn't.

And now, you see, it's quite simple when I think about it rationally. I promised Doris it would be me and her. We don't need other people in our life. Other people always make things messy. I know how this ends. Broken furniture, broken bones, broken souls. Poor Doris embroiled in a custody battle.

And I just want to save Kat from all that, you know? Be her staffie. Or like, just wrap myself around her and cushion her from all the horridness in the world. Even if there's the slightest chance that that horridness is because of me. I don't want it to wreck her, to hurt her. She's just, well, too good for that. Too good for me.

There's no point fooling myself. I've got to end it while we're still in one piece. It's for the best. I look down at her sleeping next to me. Doris is awake and giving off a low whine from beside the bed. 'Kat?' I give her a nudge. She yawns, blinks, stretches, her eyes still half closed. She pulls the sheets up over her shoulders, comes in closer to me as life last night never happened, and falls right back asleep. I pull away.

It's a conversation I just don't know how to have. I wriggle slowly out of her grip, slide out the sheets and sit on the edge of the bed. Doris is looking at me beseechingly. She knows what I'm about to do, and does not approve. I ignore her. Traitor. She's so fickle, a walk down Portobello beach and a sausage or two will cheer her up in no time. There will be others, I suppose. I mean, not like her obviously, with her picnic baskets and lemon slices and Delia Smith. But it's for the best. No attachments. No dependencies. Bish bosh on to the next. Just as I'm about to get up, gather my things together and sneak out, I feel a hand catch my wrist.

'I'm sorry about last night,' she says. 'Whenever you're ready to talk, I'm here. And whatever it is…' She pauses. 'I love you, you know?' The words are awkward in her mouth, the unfamiliarity of them. Like she's saying them for the first time.

And I feel lightheaded, dizzy, like I'm hearing her voice from underwater. My throat is dry, my tongue swollen and sticky with morning breath. And her big eyes are fixed on me with a question, just like that day on Calton Hill, before we kissed.

A beam of Saturday morning sunlight shines in past the lavender curtains in her room, and I can see shimmery dust float this way and that, and time has slowed down, so it's all in slow motion. And I think I'll just tell her that she shouldn't love me, that I'm no good. But instead, before I can stop myself, I'm telling her all sorts, that I'm sorry too, and that my dad isn't a very nice man, and I'm just scared, and I love her. And Doris is planting big licks on my feet, super happy, and Kat is rubbing her eyes, and I think I've got something in mine as well, and the next thing you know, we're trotting out happily for a walk along the beach, with sausages and sandwiches and Earl Grey in a flask, all tucked neatly into that very same picnic basket, and it all feels somehow, just right.

We are all made of stars
ROHAN KAR

Matching moons in the water signs of Pisces and Scorpio had brought them together. At least that was what Dr Patel, Rupinder's GP had told Rupinder's mother when he'd matched her with Kevin that fateful day. Rupinder had gone in to have a sore throat checked out and had left with a potential marriage mate!

They were standing in Dr Patel's surgery, when he pulled out his astrological charts and laid them ceremoniously on the patient's examination bench with a dramatic display of hands. Patel had very long fingers. In fact, one of them had already been down Rupinder's throat. He was over six foot tall, but extremely thin. Dr Patel, it seemed, was driven by a secret calling higher than his Hippocratic oath; to bring disparate souls together to the heart beat of the cosmos. All for a small fee. And Rupinder's mother was a sucker for the stars.

'I have consulted the planets and *yogas* and he is most certainly the best match,' Patel said, staring down at the charts. Patel specialised in a form of Indian astrology more ancient than seen in the West. Rupinder's mother nodded sagely, following his every word. She was dressed in a green sari in tune with her sign of Gemini. She was rather fat, and her mouth was open as she nodded, her asthmatic wheezing clearly audible. Rupinder couldn't see the sense of it all. But her mother insisted.

Rupinder had become disillusioned with the whole dating game. It was all so random and her choices had never worked out. She was nearing thirty and had come to doubt her own judgement in men.

'*Saturn's return*, when all will change,' her mother said. Perhaps she was right, Rupinder thought. All this time, she had let her heart rule her mind, but why not allow this ancient science of the stars to find her match? What harm could there be? And so she listened dutifully.

'It is quite by accident that I came across him, one of my patients. I noticed his birth date on his hospital records and sensed somehow that the natal planets might match. When I did the calculations my instinct turned out to be correct. There are some *malefic* aspects: the man has a need for excessive attention and your daughter an excess to generosity, but despite this an excellent synastry all around,' Patel smiled, his small immaculate teeth gleaming.

'Oh that is so wonderful,' Rupinder's mother wheezed. 'We have been waiting such a long time. When can my Rupinder meet him?'

'I will arrange it. The boy is quite in my confidence. He is an ex-soldier. I am treating him for an old war wound. But there is one problem.'

'What is it doctor?'

'He is a white man, an Englishman. Kevin Baldwin. But you must not fret. The planets, my dear, are never wrong.'

Some days later, when they first met Kevin at the surgery, her mother looked up at him.

'My, you're tall.'

Kevin flashed a brilliant smile and in that single moment, she was convinced.

Rupinder looked closely at Kevin's face, his high brow and long Roman nose, and his clear blue eyes. Their sparkle made her think of something crystalline and maybe a little cold. But Kevin was handsome with powerful shoulders and he spoke so well. He too had been keen to go along with Patel's introduction.

'You always trust your doctor, right?' Kevin laughed.

'Scorpio rising as well,' her mother said afterwards as they walked home in the rain. 'Dr Patel is right. He *is* the perfect match for you.'

And that was how it was. Within a few months, they were dating. Kevin would call her 'Roops' and he'd smell fresh, like lemons. She enjoyed the roughness of his skin and when they first made love in his flat, she wore red lipstick - just as he wanted her to - though she never asked why. She'd had others before, which she'd hidden from her parents, which was not surprising. They'd told her nothing of how to deal with men, or how to avoid them.

But Kevin knew the first time they'd made love. She was scared, at first wondering what his reaction would be. He just stayed inside her, lying on top, saying nothing. She could feel his heart beating and his smoky breath thick on the side of her neck. Her feeling for him was like an instinct, the only man who'd made her feel complete.

Within a year, they were married. Her father hadn't wanted her to marry Kevin, but she'd already become pregnant with Maya. Her father's eyes had rolled up to the ceiling when she'd told him. She saw the whites only and thought he was going to faint.

'Why you want to go through with this?' he asked her. 'You could do so much more. He is a taxi driver. And he is white. Their culture is different. They are used to taking things. Just look at the past.'

'I love him bapu. And ammi has seen him in the stars. He is right for me. I can't explain it.'

She sees her father now in her mind's eye, huddled at a small sewing machine in the living room of her childhood home. His movement skilful and intelligent, but frustrated, as if he could have done something more. It is a big room filled with the clutter of a small life. Forty years ago, he'd started like this, an Indian immigrant, a tailor from Tamil Nadu, who arrived shivering at Southampton docks on the SS Arcadia on a cold February morning with a small leather suitcase and a sewing machine. He'd worked hard in every sense: 'You know, when the time came for me to marry, my mother arranged it all from Madras!'

Sometimes her parents helped out. Within a year of Maya's birth, Little Jonny came along. She didn't like to ask, but there had been moments when she'd been so desperate she could do little else. Kevin was a hard man, ten years as a squaddie in the Queens Regiment, he'd seen action in Belize, Kosovo and Belfast. She'd only just found out that his time away had also included a short spell in prison. The old war wound Patel had mentioned had never healed: the wound was in the mind. It left Kevin's behaviour, unpredictable, violent. His small minicab firm begun to fail.

It was hard for her father seeing her like this, living in a council flat in a part of the city long forgotten. She felt his concern keenly, the pain of a father not yet done.

Now with Maya and Little Jonny sleeping next door, she stared at a photograph of Kevin. It was four years since their marriage and he had begun to show his age, He would mourn her absence from their home, with no one to cook or clean, to remove his washed underpants from the radiators, to put away his black boots or throw away his half-smoked rollups. And yet only a few months ago, when she'd been in hospital for a hysterectomy, he had visited her daily, each time bringing with him a single red carnation. Her father had been careful to leave just before Kevin's arrival, always leaving before he came.

She looked at the photograph, still in her hands, with an awful loneliness and suddenly felt her mother's absence, an infallible, unfailing force. At times, she thinks her mother is near and talking, but that she just can't hear her. She sees her in her mind's eye, dressed in a sari, silent and still in the coffin in the living room of her parents home.

Rupinder put down the frame – so Kevin's face couldn't be seen. Tears pricked her eyes.

It will be all right, she's certain her mother whispers in her ear. *Don't be afraid.*

Rupinder knew this must be true, for her mother had always spoken the truth.

She found another photo hidden inside an old cloth case that Kevin had brought from his previous flat. It was in the loft when she'd gone up there to put some old toys away.

She could sense her mother beside her, guiding her way. It was dusty, cool and damp. The light was weak and she'd stumbled into a pile of empty, cardboard boxes, knocking them over, revealing the faded green vanity case.

Open it, she hears.

The photo was of a pretty girl with blonde hair, large eyes and a small, red, lipsticked mouth. There was a playfulness in her blue eyes. It was signed: 'Love, Coreen. Belfast, Summer 1996.' She'd put it in her pocket, and downstairs, after staring at it and turning the photo over and over in hands that were moist with sweat, Rupinder had left it on the bed face down for Kevin to see.

'*What's this?*' he said, when he returned from work. It was late and the children were already in bed.

'I found it in the attic,' she said, apprehensively, not quite sure how he would react. He picked up the photo, turned it around and then she saw his expression darken.

'Who is she Kevin?'

He looked at her with a vicious, intense gaze. 'Don't ask. It's got nothing to do with you.'

'What do you mean, I'm your wife!'

'Leave me alone,' he shouted.

'Kevin, the children. Keep your voice down. What's the matter with you?'

Suddenly Kevin jumped out of bed and slapped her hard across the face such that her head flipped back, and she fell against the wall. She felt him bear down upon her, like an animal out for murder. Without thinking, she immediately ran from the room slamming the door behind her and holding her stinging cheek.

The next day after Kevin had left for work, she packed her bags. He had not spoken a single word, but she knew he felt guilty. All day she had been going back and forth torn between leaving or not, but finally she'd called her father to come and collect her, and he was waiting now, downstairs with the children, although she couldn't see his car.

It was getting dark and soon Kevin would return to an empty flat. How could she put up with his violence? She didn't want to call the police as he'd already been in trouble. But she was scared. She looked out of the window to the car park. Without her husband, it would be hard bringing up the kids alone. Maya, who is normally close to her, has suddenly been getting angry for no reason, screaming at her in the shops or at the bus stop. Jonny will suffer most, he'd always followed Kevin around like a small, lost duckling; holding up his arms to be carried and talking with such a tiny voice. *His asthma might get worse*, she thought suddenly.

She was downstairs at last and her father lowers the electric window of the car. '*Where have you been?*' he shouts. 'Where's all your stuff?' his voice shakes as he speaks, betraying the fear she knows he is trying hard to conceal.

Streetlight refracted off the shiny top of the car into blades of coloured light.

Rupinder shook herself awake – she'd forgotten her remaining bags. She had a sense of her mother's voice and that she was talking. *What am I doing?*

'I'm sorry, Dad,' she said quickly and then hesitated, looking up at the small window of her flat. It seemed so very high and far away, like a reflecting fragment of Rapunzel's tower.

"I'll… I'll get them now, Dad,' she said. 'There's only four bin bags. Wait here – I'll just be a minute.'
Rupinder climbed the stairs quickly, telling herself that she was stupid, that her father was right, that her whole life has proved him right.

At the top of the stairs, she stopped at the flat's front door, thinking that she heard a rustle from inside. Her heart pounded in her chest, but as she pushed the door open she saw that all was the same.

It will be all right.

Her eyes were playing tricks on her. The bags were still on the floor where she'd left them. She felt herself breathe again and moved quickly, lifting them easily. Then she paused, staring at the letter on the table – it's as she left it; she heard the soft ticking off the Swiss clock. Kevin had given it to her as a Christmas present in their first year together. He was good then and seemed so smart, the kind who'd get on in life.

Her eyes welled with shame; she was leaving the only home her children had ever known.

Her chest felt tight, but then she turned, squeezing the bags hard against herself. She pushed open the door and let it close with a dry, metallic click. The corridor is dark and silent apart from the muffled noise of the Somali children playing next door. They will be sad to see her go.

Outside, a cold wind bit at her face. And then, she saw *him*. Kevin was leaning over the bonnet of her father's car, his hands, like spiders laden with gold, were spread wide over the metal body. Her father stared motionless at her through the windscreen and her heart quickened.

Kevin turned his head, his warrior's brown hair down to his shoulders, his breath came in short wispy puffs. He saw her and next he eyed the bags. She knew then she was right to leave.

'What the fuck's going on?' he shouted, the veins in his temples jumping.

'Kevin… we *must* go.'

His expression changed into a smile; the same brilliant smile that she first saw at Patel's surgery and the words of her ma ringing in her ears: *We are all made of stars.*

She put the bags down and opened her handbag, taking out a small black container which she threw to the tarmac by his feet. He stared at the broken, shattered lipstick; red gunge oozed from the cracks in the road.

'No! I need you, Roops,' he pleaded, quickly looking up. 'You can't go… I promise I'll change. She was a Catholic -

from the wrong side of town. And worse, she was already married! It ended my career. A month later, she left me.'

Rupinder stood still watching him, but as if from a great distance.

'Roops, that was a long time ago,' Kevin shouts, holding out his hands. 'I'm a different man now. You turned my life around, right? You lifted me from the gutter and I... love you – I never loved her, not like I love you!'

He walked around the side of the car and peered into the side window. The children laughed and waved. Jonny put his face to the window, smearing the glass with sticky, milky-brown fingers.

'Jonny, son,' Kevin shouted through the window. 'Come out, come out to Daddy - and bring your sister with you.'

'No, Kevin, don't...' she begged, but Jonny had already stepped out of the car and moved towards his father, his little head looked up, his arms held high.

She was lost – not in her thoughts but lost to him, her once white knight. This is all she knew, all she had. And yet, was there still a chance?

Rupinder Baldwin lifted her son up in her arms, cradling him and nodded to her father who nervously took the cases from the car.

She didn't see the tears in her father's eyes as he drove away, Maya having joined her brother in the still night air.

Rupinder looked up at the sky. It seemed to stare back at her, fully black and jewelled with bright, twinkling stars.

Soul Sisters
RESHMA RUIA

Suman Bakshi rents a room on a quiet street in West Didsbury. She has grey eyes. She works as a filing clerk at the Platt textile museum, a rundown red brick converted mill that squats on the outskirts of the city, just beyond the roar of the M 56 motorway. The work is slow. Few people can be bothered to climb down the twenty steps to her basement office where she keeps the records on Eighteenth century spinning and weaving practises. She has plenty of time to read her novels, file her nails, or tweeze out stray eyebrow hairs in a small magnifying mirror she hides in her desk drawer.

But on this particular day Suman has been busy fielding queries from an American researcher who wants to know about the impact of imported Indian cotton on Lancashire mills. 'Well, there was Gandhi's boycott of British clothing...' she hesitates. Her knowledge of Indian history is threadbare. She blames her mother for the gaps in her knowledge, for insisting that the best way of assimilating in England was to memorise the names of Henry V111's beheaded wives rather than know about Gandhi's Dandi salt march for India's Independence.

Nipping out for a sandwich at lunch, Suman spots a man hunched over an ATM in the corner. She knows it is Ashok. He has the same stooping shoulders and dark hair that turns henna red when the sun hits it. She quite liked the chameleon colour change, said it made him look like a Bollywood hero. The man, his back still to her, stuffs the money in his back pocket and walks rapidly down a side street towards the railway station. She keeps up with him as far as she can, until he disappears down a set of steps. But it's not Ashok. How can it be? He has moved down south, to Cheltenham with a new woman, an Englishwoman who now shares his life and watches him snore night after night. She leaves work earlier than usual, hurries home, changes into her blue velour track suit with its faded bleached back pocket and her fluffy Disney slippers. Cuddling a bowl of Maggi chicken curry noodles, she slumps on the sofa with a book. It is Suman's third reading of Narshida Malik's novel, *The Nightingale of Kansas*. The bruised cover shows a blindfolded bird inside a cage. A few pages are folded into little origami fans with entire passages highlighted in yellow. The scribbled comments and underlined passages are the milestones by which she navigates her life. 'Unfeeling brutes,' she writes on page fifty-five, straight after this:

'The boys came up to me as I waited in the queue at Macdonald's. 'Aren't you boiling in this Mrs Osama Bin Laden? What are you-a letterbox? How will you post the burger? They shouted as I pushed past them and ran home, their spit hanging on my niqab. They made me feel ashamed to be me.' (Page 55, *'The Nightingale of Kansas'*)

Suman underlines the last line and stops reading.

She closes her eyes, sinks back on the bed, the book nestling between her breasts and remembers. It was a warm July. A Saturday. The heat was like a razor blade slicing her skin. She was at the Arndale centre, window shopping. Hot and sticky, she'd bought herself an ice-cream cone. Peanut brittle and Vanilla. A gaggle of school boys, satchels slapping against their thighs, snorted as they walked past her. 'Percy Piiiig…' Their voices still ring in her ear. At forty two, she is still surprised by the careless cruelty of the human male.

Suman sighs, gets up and walks to the fridge. She is hungry again. There is a Tupperware container with leftover dal and rice. She eats it cold, her back pressed against the thrumming front of the fridge. The spoon diving in and out of the container until it is empty. She thinks about calling her mother, telling her about how she'd almost seen Ashok and lost him. But she decides against it.

'Wake up, Suman. Stop day dreaming and hiding in them bloody books,' Is what her mother would say.

#

Ashok had walked out on her fortieth birthday, leaving her stranded at the George and Dragon, alone with her half-finished lemonade. It was the royal wedding and their local was strung up with red and blue union jacks and men spilling on to the pavements gripping pints of lager. Women stood together, mouths knit in cautious dreamy smiles. The pub had put up a giant screen in the car park and there was much oohing over the bridesmaid's dress. Suman had felt quietly proud standing in the car park, staring at the confetti on the screen, proud to be sharing her birthday with royalty.

Ashok had told her to come inside.

'We'll miss the wedding vows,' she complained as she followed him. All the tables were empty, but Ashok led her to the farthest one, the one near the Ladies. Stupidly she had thought he was going to give her a surprise gift. He knew she had her eyes on an Omega watch.

'The thing is, Suman,' Ashok said. 'I don't think I'm in love with you anymore.'

His hands lay flat on the oak table, and he was studying his fingers as though they were arrows telling him which way to run.

A roar came from outside and Suman wasn't sure if the crowd was cheering Ashok or Prince William.

She spent the rest of the afternoon sitting on the toilet, her head in her hands.

He had found someone else. It was as simple as that.

#

The room is dark. Suman switches on the television. She needs the noise and the flicker of light. The news is on. Another bomb explosion in Kabul or maybe it is Baghdad, she can't be sure. She stares at the images. It is like a video game, the streaks of light shooting against the dark of the sky. She hopes Narshida is okay, even though she knows Narshida lives in America, but one can never tell with writers. Their research can lead them anywhere. Especially a woman like Narshida- at times Suman feels that every word she reads is written with a pen dipped in blood.

Narshida's photo is taped on her wardrobe mirror. She'd found the photograph in an out of date issue of Time magazine at the dentist's. The picture reveals a woman with troubled eyes. Her mouth is full and dark. Suman imagines it painted a crimson red. She walks up to the photo and strokes the deep lines running down the sides of the mouth. She has similar lines. She runs a thumb down the sides of her nose. There they are, like a railway track.

'Do something Suman, slap on some foundation, some lipstick,' her mother said after Ashok's exit. 'You've got to look young to find another man.'

And Suman did try. She went to Debenhams, pulled out Narshida's picture from her bag and told the gum-chewing girl at the makeup counter. 'Make me like her.' But she came back home the same.

#

It began quietly, the love affair with Narshida Malik. Suman had visited the local library one afternoon, her winter coat hiding her fleecy pyjamas. She stood bewildered in front of a shelf of books until the librarian, Mrs Jones came up to her and placing a hand on her shoulder, asked if she needed help.

'Do you have any instruction manuals on how to be happy? Some sort of Do-It-Yourself guide?' Suman did her best to force back the tears, gulped hard and told herself she wasn't going to cry.

'Why would you need such a book, my dear?' Mrs Jones voice reminded Suman of black and white films.

'We're not engines that need fixing,' the woman continued. And Suman's eyes had welled up at such unexpected kindness.

Mrs Jones handed her a box of tissues.

'But then again, I may have just the book for you. You will adore, *The Red Rose of Kabul*' by Narshida Malik. She is a foreigner like you, but she is very clever. Every word is written in English and it falls like a tear drop,' Mrs Jones said, walking briskly to the shelf at the farthest corner of the library.

'What is it about?' Suman asked politely, her eyes scanning the shelves for a book with a bold, chirpy cover, something like, 'How to Win friends and Influence People.'

'It's about a woman whose husband abandons her and goes off to war,' Mrs Jones said, her eyes glinting inside her red framed spectacles. 'That's men for you…forever chasing skirts and glory,' she added, handing Suman the book like a gift.

Suman wondered if Ashok was seeking glory and not a skirt when he walked out on her.

She read through the novel in one sitting, rooting every step of the way for Noor, the proud protagonist who defied tradition.

'Life did not have to end just because your man walked out the door, the seasons still changed; she still had a brain and a healthy body.'
(pg. 70, *The Red Rose of Kabul*)

She copied out the words in her notebook. And once finished, went back for some more. In six months Suman had read through the library's entire collection of Narshida Rashid's books.

She writes to Narshida's publisher in New York. The letters come back unanswered.

Suman files them carefully in chronological order.

'It won't be long before Narshida visits England. I can feel it in my bones,' she confides in Mrs Jones. The two women have become close. Not friends exactly, but they sometimes share a coffee at the Costa on Wednesdays when the library is closed.

'I'm sure I heard something about a book tour on Radio Four, but I could be mistaken,' Mrs Jones replies and passes her, 'The Tears for the Unknown.'

'Keep up with your reading and stay well clear of men. They ought to come with a health warning,' she says, squeezing Suman's arm.

#

A month later she receives a telephone call. It's her brother.

'How's life, Suman?' He asks his voice Cola-light. He doesn't really care. She knows that. They are siblings, but their planets spin on different axis. And on her part she doesn't begrudge him his glitter-happy life as a young man earning good money in the city.

'The usual stuff, Jai' she replies and waits.

'Are you sure you've not got your head buried in one of them…Arab woman's books?'

She can hear his snigger down the telephone line.

'Narshida is of Afghan heritage, not Arab. She spells out the distinction carefully.

'Well, guess which Arab chick is coming to town,' Jai says.

#

Suman rings in sick the next day and spends the day hunting for a new dress. She settles on a silk dress with a scarlet and black roses print. On her way home, she stops by the library and shows the dress to Mrs Jones, lifting it out of its tissue wrapping like a magician pulling a rabbit out of a hat.

'Fit for a bride, not that you'd want to be repeating that mistake again, my dear,' Mrs Jones says. 'I bet it cost a fortune.'

'I wanted the best,' Suman replies. 'How else will Narshida know it's me?'

She is travelling to London to meet Narshida who is on a whistle-stop tour to launch her new book.

Suman reaches Euston and calls her brother. He can't meet her, 'Important stuff at the office. Some of us have to work for a living you know.'

She imagines him at his desk: shoulders tense, face pushed against a computer screen.

'Your ticket for the reading will be waiting at the box office,' he says.

The rest of her day is a blur. She has a vague memory of crowds rushing past, the orange marmalade of the sun spread thinly across the sky. At some point she must have been hungry, she remembers the mushroom pizza at the Pizza Hut by Trafalgar square, the Cath Kidston tote crammed full of books digging into her hip.

She is early for the book launch. She orders a bottle of Shiraz, a packet of crisps and opens her notebook and begins to write.

Question one for Narshida: 'Can I persuade you to hold a reading in Manchester? There is a lovely old lady from the local library. She is a fan too. Maybe I will even cook for you. My ex-husband Ashok loved my cooking.'

Question two…

When she looks up, the bottle is empty and there is a queue outside the auditorium.

'Excuse me, excuse me…yes, family …friend of the author…special reserved seat…special needs,' she shouts, pushing past people, breathless by the time she gets to her seat.

Jai hasn't got her a front row ticket. But at least she has a clear, unrestricted view of the stage.

'Narshida's late. Isn't she? But then she is the star of the show.' She turns companionably to her neighbour, a bespectacled girl who scowls and mutters something inaudible.

#

Lights dim. Silence falls. A short haired woman comes on stage and takes the microphone. Suman wants the crowd to stop snivelling and shuffling and scratching. The woman taps on the mic to make sure it's working. A crackle echoes throughout the room.

'Ladies and gentlemen welcome to an evening with Narshida Malik....' She clears her throat and explains that Narshida is in the middle of a global world tour launching her new book. Film rights have already been bought by Angelina Jolie.

Suman edges forward in her seat, her knees squashed together.

'That's my girl,' she whispers, her chest swelling in pride.

The crimson velvet curtains part and there she is, standing before her. Just for her. Narshida's head is covered with a brown silk scarf and a turquoise necklace shines across her chest. The crowd starts clapping but Suman stays silent. Her hands are shaking as she lifts her camera and stands up. Murmurs of disapproval rise around her.

Narshida is staring at her, framed in her lens, her black hooded eyes -still and mysterious. The interviewer stands up from her chair and grabs the mic.

'Please, no photographs. Narshida doesn't like the flash.'

The interview begins. Suman leans forward, tilts her head so she can listen clearly. She hears an American voice as Narshida reads aloud, flicking through the pages of her new novel, *The Nightmare of Baghdad.'*

'I won't let you go out without wearing the hijab. What will the world say? Nadia shook her head. You are my brother, not my protector. I will dress and live how I want…'

A woman starts clapping. Narshida silences her with a raised hand and continues. Suman is listening but the words dance inside her head.

Looking around she sees rapt hands move across paper jotting down phrases. She too should be noting down Narshida's words, instead she is sweating and fidgeting. She blames the two hour train journey and the wine.

The reading finishes. Narshida closes her book and turns to the interviewer.

'I won't be taking any personal questions, so please don't ask me about my dog, my lover or the kind of flowers I like to smell.'

The crowd titters. Suman's hand shoots up. The boy with the roving mic walks towards her. His purple tee shirt says he is against dolphin fishing.

The insides of Suman's thighs stick together, damp with sweat. Her breath is sour. The moment to shine has arrived. She knows her question: 'Narshida, are you happy? Do you ever get homesick for love?'

But Narshida's American voice, her elegant clothes and the way she drapes herself over her chair makes her question sound foolish.

'Do you have a question?' The interviewer frowns. The mic hovers over Suman's face like a missile. She opens her mouth and sneezes.

Suman sits down, head bowed, listening to the others. There are questions about Narshida's writing. A man shyly admits he's doing his PhD research on her. Narshida nods and lifts her hand to cover a yawn.

#

It is over. People rush outside to form an orderly queue for the signing. Suman takes her place, her tote unzipped, full of books waiting to be signed. It is clear to her that she needs to be alone with Narshida. Only then can they reveal their true vulnerable selves to each other.

The organiser hands out post it notes for the crowd to write out their names.

'Only one name, one book, no personal messages,' she announces. 'Narshida has a BBC interview right after. Please don't delay her.'

Suman writes her name and scribbles, 'Please meet me for a coffee, Narshida. We have so much pain in common. We are soul sisters.'

It takes her forty-five minutes to reach the table where Narshida sits, pen poised.

Suman places the novels in front of Narshida like corpses awaiting resurrection. Narshida signs one, pushes away the rest, including the note. Suman leans forward.

'I want you to read my message. Read it now please.'
Narshida gives her a quick look and frowns.

'I don't have time. Can you see the queue?' She looks beyond Suman's shoulder.

'Next please.'

'There is no next please. You have to promise to meet me. We have a lot of catching up to do.' Suman is pleading now, still leaning on the table, her bulk hiding Narshida from the others. She must have raised her voice because the short haired woman who seems to be the organiser is moving towards her.

'What is the problem?'

Suman smiles. She finds it funny, all this fuss over a simple message.

'I just want my sister to read my note,' she says. 'That's all. She knows me.'

Narshida starts laughing. Her teeth crowding her mouth are small and uneven.

'What sisters…Do I even fucking know you?' She picks up Suman's note and tears it up.

Tiny pieces scatter on the table like confetti.

'Will you please move away madam? Otherwise I will have to call security.' The organiser's hand is on Suman's shoulder, nudging her out of the way.

#

The hall empties, but Suman waits by the door for Narshida to finish her BBC interview. A cleaner arrives, driving a little motorized hoover. Suman blocks his way, forcing him to stop.

'Are you all right, lady?'

'It's nice being called a lady,' she says. 'I just wanted to tell you that Narshida didn't mean to be rude. She was just jetlagged and tired, that's all.'

The cleaner looks confused so Suman waves him off.

She checks her watch. She's missed the last train home.

She sees Narshida, hurrying out of a side door, head bowed, deep in conversation with another woman. They walk quickly towards the exit. Suman follows them. Couples walk past, heads lowered, hands entwined, the click of their heels like a wedding march.

A thousand stars scar the sky.

A road appears. The woman beside Narshida hails a cab. They shake hands and she disappears. Narshida is alone. She crosses the road, lifting a hand to halt the cars and the buses. She has removed her head scarf and Suman sees that her hair is long and dark. She would like to run her fingers through her hair. Maybe Narshida will gift her a lock, a little memento of their meeting. The hair will carry her scent. Suman stops, she feels light headed. Her mobile rings. It's her brother. She lets it ring out.

Narshida is still walking and Suman steps up her pace, breathless by the time she catches up with her. But not quite. Narshida is still quicker. She enters a glass building with revolving doors. Suman looks up to read the sign. All that grand talk about a movie deal and she is only staying in a three star Mercure hotel. She would have to tell Mrs Jones about it. Why, if she had her way, she'd have booked Narshida a suite at the Ritz.

Suman walks into the hotel lobby, head bowed, rummaging through her bag, as though looking for a room key. A group of American tourists are at the check in desk, clutching maps and iPads. She sidles up behind them, waiting her turn.

'I am here to meet Miss Narshida Malik…an interview. I'm from the Museum of…' She flashes her staff card at the receptionist who is jabbing the computer in front of him, while answering the phone. He is young with a freckled face and a badge that says, 'Training.'

'Room 435.' He doesn't even look at her.

A Japanese couple are waiting for the lift. The girl, pale and slim, dressed in jeans and a tee shirt with little teddy bears embroidered in rhinestone.

'I like your tee shirt. It's cute,' Suman tells the girl once they are inside the lift. The couple bow together, their heads almost touching.

'You must be on your honeymoon. You like London?' But she doesn't wait for their answer because the doors open, her floor is there.

#

The night turns dark. The streets empty of people. A cyclist in a high visibility yellow jacket cycles past the short overweight woman walking towards the river.

She meant no harm. If only the stupid girl hadn't tried to shout. If only she had sat quietly on the bed and listened to her story. But no, Narshida had to act funny. Why couldn't she stop screaming? The only way to keep her quiet was to put the pillow to her face. There was stillness then. And Suman could finally tell her about Ashok. And smoke her cigarette. And tell her how much she loved her books.

Suman leans on the railing, watching the river, sleek and shiny with night time lights.

The bag with the unsigned books cuts into her shoulder. She opens her bag and lets the books slip out into the waters below. They fall quietly, without making the slightest splash.

Entwined Destinies
SHIBANI LAL

'The soul is healed by being with children'
- Fyodor Dostoevsky

Papa watches her sleep; a sad smile slowly forms upon his furrowed countenance. In a week she will no longer be with him, and although this is exactly what he has wanted for her, he cannot free himself of the thought that tugs at his very core – is this really what she wants?

He coughs, a harsh raspy sound and looks over at her worriedly; he doesn't want her to wake up. But she sleeps on, soundly as she has always done. He remembers the first time he cradled her in his arms, that fateful night nearly eighteen years ago, when, after a long and difficult labour, the little girl's first breath coincided with her mother's last. He remembers that feeling of hopelessness, as he looked down at the mewling bundle in his arms, unsure of what to feel, of what to do. He coughs again, louder this time; he feels an unpleasant rattle deep in his chest.

There was a time when Papa slept like her – dead to the world, back when life offered much promise, and opportunity was his for the taking. He was young and excitable then, his head in the clouds: life was a series of magical afternoons spent fantasizing about his future in

London, filled with dreams of immersing himself in the city's magic and beauty as he walked down the narrow cobbled streets. The threat of the London cold didn't faze him, conversely, he yearned to feel the icy tentacles of the winter wind clawing at his face, only to be thawed by the warmth of the spring sunshine.

Papa shakes his head impatiently, almost as though to displace the thoughts from his head. With a soft grunt and with significant effort, he hoists himself from his chair and hobbles over to his bedroom, across the hallway.

#

It was the summer of 1980. Five years earlier, his father and uncle, *Bada-Papa* and *Chachu* took a giant leap of faith, pooling their meagre savings to open up a small store opposite the Gateway of India, the centre of tourist Bombay. The rather unimaginatively named *Bombay Handicraft Boutique* opened sans fanfare, but they enjoyed great success selling colourful trinkets and handicrafts sourced from across the country, which, over a relatively short period allowed them to trade in their cramped one-bedroom home for a moderately spacious two-bedroom flat off Grant Road, where, nestled amongst the whores and diamond merchants – the Dayal brothers felt they had finally arrived.

Bada-papa was far too involved with the running of the store to worry much about his son. Although like all fathers, he harboured an innate desire to have Papa manage the business after he and the bachelor *Chachu* retired, he knew this was not to be. The boy was too soft; his passions lay elsewhere. He could draw, it was all he did and he was fascinated by buildings – tall, cramped, towering and squat; he drew them all, capturing intricate details so masterfully, that *Bada-papa* couldn't, despite his inherent disappointment, bear to waste the boy's talent by asking him to accompany them as they haggled with Rajasthani craftsmen for their wares. So he encouraged the boy to draw and upon the advice of his schoolteachers, helped his son write up his application to an Architecture school in London. Upon hearing that the school has awarded Papa a place, on a full scholarship he tells his son to go to London and follow his dreams; that *Bada-papa* will work doubly-hard to cover the travel costs to London.

#

Papa is forced to defer his entry by a year, as *Bada-papa* needs time to raise the funds. He waits impatiently, sketching furiously, fired with an urgent passion; his head filled with visions of what he is about to see and what he hopes to create.

However, tragedy strikes a few short weeks before he is due to leave; his luggage neatly, expectantly stacked and labelled in the hallway: *Bada-papa* and *Chachu* are killed instantly on a trip to Gujarat, their bodies unrecognizable amongst the sea of mangled limbs and the carcass of the derailed train. Overnight, Papa finds himself bestowed with the dubious honour of being the oldest male in the family, comprising two younger sisters and a grieving widow. He is left with no choice. With the steadiest of hands he pens a note to the Admissions officer at the School, informing him in clean neat script that regretfully, due to a recent misfortune he is forced to withdraw his application and requests the school to return his portfolio at their earliest convenience.

The luggage is emptied, the cupboards are filled with winter clothes he now no longer needs, but cannot bear to return. Several weeks later, the postman delivers a heavy brown envelope to the Dayal household, littered with stamps and postmarks. Papa cannot bear to open it but does so late one night as the family sleeps, his hands trembling as he cradles his beloved sketches, allowing himself to - for the first time since the accident - weep for his loss. Finally, after hours of angst, he carefully, deliberately rips the sketches into fine shreds and sets fire to the remains in the courtyard outside the flat. He wipes his eyes as the flames greedily lick away at his dreams and wearily walks back home, the weight of the world on his young shoulders. From that day onward, the words London and Architecture are no longer mentioned in the Dayal household.

#

With a singular passion Papa throws himself into running the store, and to everyone's surprise, mainly his own, he proves to be a dab hand at managing its fortunes. The bitterness he'd felt as he'd first walked into the store after the tragedy no longer bites at his heart, he now accepts that the destiny of the store is closely entwined with his own. Using the money *Bada-papa* had saved for his journey to London, he acquires the neighbouring *Haseena's Handloom Haven*, and now oversees an empire encompassing traditional *saris*, textiles, handicrafts and semi-precious gems sourced from across the country. He pays for his sisters' weddings, garish week-long affairs, just as they'd wanted and buys a bigger flat in the more upmarket Marine Lines, much to his mother's delight. He marries too, and for the two years before the girl's birth, they live happily: it is not a marriage filled with romance, more one of practical co-dependence. Although he didn't love his wife, he felt a certain fondness towards her and despite his mother's fervent pleading refuses to re-marry after her death, confident that he can single-handedly shower his daughter with all the love and affection she can possibly desire.

The birth of his daughter stirs up warmth and passion that Papa hasn't felt in years. Her innocence, her childish simplicity makes him feel alive, and slowly, he finds himself reverting to his boyish exuberance, delighting in her gurgles as he bounces her happily on his shoulders. Father and daughter weave a magical world of togetherness, the house echoes with laughter and love.

#

The girl is five years old. It is an otherwise unremarkable Wednesday evening; she greets Papa as she always does, running into his arms as soon as returns from work. Today however, she has something special for him – shyly, not unmixed with some pride, she hands over her gift – a drawing of them by the beach, her attempt at capturing a day out with her father several weeks ago. Two golden stars in the far right corner indicate her teacher's pleasure with her efforts. Papa stares at the piece of paper, transfixed for what seems an age. Only when the girl begins to cry – thinking mistakenly that her beloved Papa isn't happy with her drawing – does he acknowledge her. He scoops her in his arms, soothes her puffy eyes with soft buttery kisses and tells her just how much he loves her present – that it makes him feel very special. She beams at him, offering to draw him another picture. His face lights up in delight, she has never seen him so radiant before. She rushes to her room and a short while later emerges with another drawing, of a butterfly she has copied from one of her books. Papa cannot believe his eyes; he cannot believe he hasn't noticed the girl's talent before - that it has taken him so long.

Within a week, he has made arrangements for an art teacher to come home once a fortnight, to further his daughter's obvious gift. The girl enjoys her classes, learning and applying her new techniques quickly and effortlessly, much to her teacher's delight. But it is really the joy on Papa's face as she shows him her artwork that motivates her. She wins art competitions; her father displays her certificates proudly on his bedroom walls. She doesn't know it yet, but her father has grand plans for her...

It is through her art classes that she meets Arun, a gangly bespectacled boy, few years older. They share the same teacher, and since they live on the same road, Mrs. Pantaki suggests they take lessons together, thereby saving her a trip each week. It is an instant friendship, and within a few months they are inseparable, spending all their free time together. Their camaraderie continues long after Arun has swapped art classes for tennis lessons; he is now her best friend and confidante. It is to him she confesses that she doesn't care much for art; that she continues to draw because it makes Papa happy. That despite what her father thinks, despite her talent, she harbours no desire to be an artist; that she would prefer to run the store with her father. She has always loved the store, she cannot understand it but she feels the essence of her father within the store's walls, his imprint on the displays, the shop tills, and yearns to take over from her father when he retires, to protect everything he has so lovingly nurtured.

#

The girl is seventeen. She has applied for a place at a prestigious Art School in London – it was easier to send the application than to argue with the combined force of Papa and her art teachers at home and at school. Papa senses her anxiety, her diffidence and decides to ask her about it in a few days; he is too ill and weak at the moment, plagued with a horrible rickety cough that has come out of nowhere, one that shakes him at his very core.

But there is no time over the next few weeks, as Papa shuffles between the office and a series of doctor's appointments, undergoing a battery of tests.

'Nothing to worry about *beti*,' he tells her, running his hand across her cheek affectionately, tearing his eyes away from the worry that haunts hers. 'I'm just run down, tired, nothing that I will not recover from in a few weeks,' he reassures her confidently, but she notices that he averts his gaze as he continues to cough violently into his handkerchief. She cannot ignore the flurry of worry lines that have magically appeared, engaged in a perpetual dance across his forehead. She has also noticed that his *kurta*, once taut against his ample belly now hangs slightly loose. It is because he's had this cough for so many weeks, she reassures herself, thinking of jolly Shobha Aunty from the flat downstairs who has now regained her plump figure after losing several kilos to a particularly violent attack of bronchitis two Novembers ago. Still, doubt persists, cold and clammy, biting at her chest.

'I'm sure he'd tell you if it were something serious,' whispers Arun as he plays with her hair. 'I wouldn't worry if I were you, it's probably some virus, Bombay is so polluted these days,' he continues. She sighs, softly, leaning against his chest, tracing her fingers against the curved line of his jaw. She loves him dearly, although Papa still thinks they are good friends, as do Arun's highly conservative parents. It is easier that way.

#

It is in Arun's calming presence that she tears open the heavy brown envelope and learns that she has been awarded a place at the Art School – that term begins in three months, the first of September.

'When are you going to tell him that you don't want to go? Surely you have to tell him soon, haven't you waited long enough?' Arun asks her, fixing her with his steady gaze.

She trembles, 'Yes, soon,' she whispers. 'I'll tell him, I've been wanting to, it's just that he's so ill nowadays, I don't want to trouble him too much,' she continues.

'I don't understand,' Arun replies, 'I mean most fathers would be delighted to have their children take over the family business – are you sure he wouldn't be happy to hear you want to run the store with him?' Arun continues, perplexed. He has, much against his parent's wishes decided to train as a lawyer, despite hailing from a family of doctors.

'I don't know, I can't explain it, I just know he really wants me to go to London, it's as though he's been preparing me for this all my life,' she sighs miserably, unaware of the truth weighing down her words. Arun squeezes her hand, reassuringly, 'I'm sure he'll be happy to have you stay here, what father wouldn't? And then we can tell him about us too,' he continues happily. She sighs. She knows it is difficult for him, his parents are keen for him to marry, not a week passes without another proposal and they are tiring of his excuses. But he is waiting for her to tell Papa first, wants to ensure that Papa blesses their union before anybody else...

#

Papa is delighted upon learning of her acceptance at the Art School. He joyously distributes boxes of *laddoos* to the neighbours: is he imagining it or is the girl not as excited as he thought she would be? Perhaps she's just processing it all, he thinks; after all it is a big change. He feels reassured, although he cannot completely shake away a niggling feeling in the pit of his stomach.

A few hours before dinner, he knocks on her door, wanting to know if she is free: he wants to take her to the store, wants to show her something. The girl is intrigued. She is quiet as her father leads her into his office, softly locking the door behind him. She watches her father as he wordlessly unlocks a drawer at the bottom of his desk – pulling out a pile of papers. She gasps – they are beautiful – sketches, drawings, paintings – all done by her beloved Papa over the years, in the quiet sanctuary of his office, every day, for a few hours each afternoon.

'I started drawing again shortly after you were born,' he tells her quietly. 'You made me feel alive, made me feel like I could draw again,' he continues softly.

'But Papa, why can't you draw at home, with me?' she asks, hurt that he has felt the need to do this so clandestinely over the years.

He shakes his head. 'I cannot explain it, *beta*,' he confesses softly. 'This is the only room where I can draw, where I will ever allow myself to draw,' he replies. And then, slowly, quietly, without bitterness or emotion, Papa tells her about his youth, his dream, his passion, and of his disappointment all those years ago. The girl listens quietly, her face wet with tears as she imagines her father at her age, having to contend with the cruel hand of fate. And then she weeps for herself, burdened by the weight of what her father has told her, suddenly acutely aware of the sword of destiny hanging over her head.

He watches her quietly, unable to understand the extent of her distress. He places her hands, soft and delicate, in his and asks her softly, '*Beti*, you want to go to London don't you?' I know it is far and it is away from all you know – home, me, the store, your school friends, even your friend Arun - but it is what you want, isn't it?'

She pauses, gazing into her father's deep brown eyes, brimming with love and concern, flanked by deep creases on either side of his face. It is the opportunity she has been yearning for, but as her eyes fall upon the sketches lying on his desk, his deepest secret exposed, so raw, so real, she cannot bring herself to speak. Her tongue feels thick; she is unable to form the words in her mouth, acutely aware that in saying them, she will shatter his dreams all over again. So she says nothing, and smiles at him, clutching his hand in hers…

#

Papa is concerned by how swollen her eyes are. He knows it couldn't have been easy, saying goodbye to Arun, her best friend. He has wondered, occasionally, whether the two are more than just friends, but has assumed, that the girl would have told him if they were. Still, he is perturbed. He doesn't ask her though; perhaps he doesn't want to know? So he continues to read quietly as the girl sobs in her room, still hurting from Arun's rage, his accusation that she is being selfish, that she doesn't love him enough, and finally, that he never wants to see her again…

#

They are at the airport, she has checked-in for her flight; Papa marvels at how smart she looks, dressed in her jeans and jacket, travel documents in hand. She indulges him as he takes photos of her, using the opportunity to study her father closely. His once thick dark hair has been reduced to a few pitiful grey wisps that hang limply across his head. His *kurta* continues to sag forlornly against his once portly form. His cough still rattles within his chest; it has been so long, she now cannot remember a time when he did not cough.

The air is thick with the fragrance of rose oil – a scent he once associated with her mother, and now with her. It is more difficult than he could ever have possibly imagined.

He pulls her towards him, '*Beti*, work hard, be good, do your Papa proud,' he whispers, as tears fall down his cheeks.

'Papa, I want to…,' she begins. Maybe it's not too late to tell him, but she's lost him to a series of coughs again, and by the time he's regained his composure, she's lost hers. So she says nothing, reaching out instead for her father's hand: is it her imagination or does his hand feel frailer than it did a few weeks ago?

He rests his hand on her head tenderly, breathing in her scent, trying to capture it all, knowing that he will not have the luxury of doing this again. Because although she is due to be back in ten months for the summer break, he is almost certain he will not see her then. He doesn't expect his lungs to last long. Despite the medicines, the scans continue to disappoint and the glimmer of despair in Dr. Patel's eyes during his last check-up was impossible to ignore. He has made peace with it, grateful that he has at least lived until this day, to witness his daughter at the threshold of a new life, proud that he has succeeded in getting her this far.

'Be good, *beta*,' he repeats, kissing her on her cheeks, her forehead, her hands, unable to muster the courage to tell her that when she is back, so much will have changed. He will not be there, nor will the store. He is finalizing the sale – it should be completed in a few weeks, and then he plans to spend the rest of his days at home, reading in solace.

'Bye Papa,' she whispers wretchedly, as she walks towards the departure gates – again – she thinks of turning back and running to him, but hears him coughing weakly behind her and decides against it. So she walks on, her long confident strides masking the pain that continues to firmly grip at her chest.

He watches her walk to the gates; for an instant he is plagued with guilt, with doubt. Has he pushed her to do this? Is this what she really wants? Will his girl be happy? She looks confident, his heart swells with pride as he sees her walk away and convinces himself that he has done the right thing, this is what she wants to do... wiping his tears, Papa heads towards the exit, saying a silent prayer to *Lord Ganesha*. Almost suddenly, unconsciously, he has adopted the gait of an old man.

#

The girl continues to peer out of the window long after Bombay is reduced to a speck in the distance; turning away only once the patchy hessian canvas has completely been replaced by fluffy clouds, airy and white. She knows she has done the right thing for Papa, but only now in the confines of the aircraft does she allow herself to feel bitterness. All her life she has been a good daughter, friend, student, and gone out of her way to please others – notably Papa – not once has she done something for herself, for her own happiness. Happiness. Doesn't she owe that to herself? After all, that is what Papa really wants for her – that's why he named her *Khushi* – Hindi for happiness – isn't that what he told her all those years ago?

Khushi, she repeats softly to herself, as she drifts into a deep dreamless sleep.

By Hand
FARRAH YUSUF

Sunlight crept into his room almost as cautiously as I did. The flat was achingly familiar despite the passing of years. With each step my heart felt tighter, memories tugging it one way and reality another. Try as I might to avoid it, my eyes kept falling on the carpet. If you had not known, you would not have been able to tell, but I had known and I could tell. If you squinted you could just make out a slightly darker patch where his body had been. Left to decompose for weeks before anyone took us seriously. Various chemical concoctions masked the odour he had unknowingly left.

It was not that he had died in his home that upset me. People die in their homes the world over every day, I know that. It was the way he died. Alone. No one to miss him, no one to mourn him, no one noticing he was gone bar the landlord and his son. Me.

We had never even met. We had however corresponded, through my father for I typed all his letters, and over the years I had unwittingly painted a picture of Mr Mason through them. I only realised I had done it the day the letters stopped. Their content was mundane, routine property maintenance and financial matters, but it was their rhythm and their form that carried the scent of their sender. Mr Mason seemed to be a man of principal, for his payments were always punctual. He was reliable, for his replies to enquiries always came by return and were sent first class. He was particular, for they were always handwritten in royal blue ink using a fountain pen on lined A5 paper that he folded neatly in two. His script was elegant and his choice of language always polite but concise. Never a crossed word or a smudge, his letters were quite simply perfect. Over time the only change I ever detected was an increasing jerkiness in his pen strokes. Amongst all our progressively impersonal typed post there was something quite personal and warming about them. So much so, that I almost missed them once he was gone.

Apart from what I had deduced through his letters, all I had actually known about Mr Mason I could write on the back of an envelope. An elderly man who had made, what I had always felt was, an unusual choice for his retirement home. He lived for twelve years, and died, date as yet unknown - at least to me, in the top floor flat of a Victorian house my father had converted long ago. It was in a noisy part of north London not yet gentrified nor glamorised. We had lived there till I was fourteen when my mother declared her knees were no longer able to take the four flights of steep stairs. So when my father announced we would be moving to a leafier part of London and a retired school teacher, whose last known address was in the Welsh Valleys, would move in my mother was happy but confused.

The lower two flats always let easily, not just because they were bigger but because for their residents the proximity to the tube meant they could be in the city within twenty minutes, if that. They stayed on average two years and never really concerned themselves with their elderly neighbour who only ever nodded or wrote notes about clutter in communal areas.

One year, as I was about to print off a letter about exterior painting my father rather unexpectedly announced,

'He runs marathons'

'Who?

'Mr Mason, who else?'

'What do you mean who else? You could be talking about anyone.'

'Well we are writing to him so who else would I mean?'

The printer began to jam.

'What's wrong with it?' he asked.

'Nothing, it'll just be some stuck paper. Give me a minute. Anyway what do you mean he runs marathons?'

'I mean he runs marathons.'

'Mr Mason?'

'That's what I said isn't it?'

'But I thought you said he was in his sixties?'

'Maybe, may be seventies. It's not like I've asked him.'

'Can't you tell?'

'No I don't stare at the man. He is roundabout sixties or seventies.'

'That's a big range.'

'Not really.'

'So what... he runs them like - like now?'

'Yes.'

'That's odd.'

'Why?'

'Well he is old.'

'Old or not he runs them. We spoke today. I went to fix the front gate. He was wearing funny shorts and a big backpack and when he saw me he said it.'

'Maybe he lied because he was embarrassed by his shorts.'

'I doubt it. Says it's his sixth.'

'Sixth!'

'Likes to keep fit, clearly.'

Just as abruptly as he had started the conversation he was bored with it and we moved on to discussing the paper jam.

Unlike me, my father never queried Mr Mason's preferences.   When Mr Mason requested permission for extra bolts on his door my father arranged it. When he broke the intercom system by trying to silence it my father installed a new one with volume control. When he disconnected his landline my father simply shifted to post. For relatively urgent matters they had evolved their own system that combined notes and post. My father would put a note through his door by early afternoon and Mr Mason's reply would come by post in the morning. Through this they would agree a time my father or builders could visit. At the appointed time - never earlier, never later - my father would knock, wait, knock again, say his full name and then the bolt would jolt.

On returning from one such meeting, my father seemed perplexed.

'Maybe when one of the lower flats becomes vacant I'll offer it to Mr Mason.'

'If he wanted one of those wouldn't he ask? It's not like they haven't become vacant a dozen times since he moved into his.'

'Maybe but I think I'll suggest it. Maybe. He looked... Not, not so well. Those stairs can't help.'

'Get a lift installed.'

'Only you would say that. Where am I going to install a lift in that house?'

'Just saying.'

'Well don't. I'll suggest it next time one is vacant.'

There never was a next time.

In early December, Mr Mason and my father's communication system failed for the first time. At first we thought Mr Mason may be away.

After two weeks we began to mumble our concerns and tentatively put a note under his door.

After three weeks as our concern grew so did the number of notes.

'Sorry, just checking you are ok?' they all said in varying ways.

By week four we tried knocking unannounced. A first.

It turned out that none of the neighbours had seen him but many had been away over the holidays. The height of the house meant you could not see into the flat's windows easily. Perhaps he is just away for Christmas we kept saying.

But by week five we began calling social services and the police.   The calls usually faltered on data protection or went round in circles.

'Are you a relative?'

'No.'

'Are you a friend?'

'No.'

'Are you a neighbour?'

'No.'

'Well how do you know him?'

'He is a tenant.'

'So you have key?'

'Yes but it will be bolted from inside.'

'How do you know that?'

'Just. We are sure he always bolts it. Besides if he is ok we don't want to scare him.'

'So you think he is ok?

'I don't know but I think it is more likely he isn't.'

'And what makes you think he isn't? No one else has reported it.'

The circles only ended when I used two magic words together.

'Vulnerable' and 'smells'.

The first was true, I felt, but the second was not. Well at least not then.

As soon as I uttered them, I knew I had broken the code. The glacial pace of the call shifted to speeding. Suddenly officers would be there in fifteen minutes but I must bring the keys. I told them we needed forty-five as we now lived on the other side of the north circular. Within the hour they were in. Bolts broken. Our notes lay unopened. Once touched, the stench of rotten flesh hurtled through the house like a fire. Somehow within hours they managed to extinguish it.

In the days that followed, we were given details of Mr Mason's next of kin. My father called to ask if they would like to collect his personal belongings. My appetite for information was greater than his and I could not stop myself from eavesdropping. All I could establish however was that Mr Mason's sister kept saying sorry. The initial call ended quickly but a few hours later she called back. Keen to explain that Mr Mason had never given her his address. Claiming it was simpler that way. So they corresponded, occasionally, through a mailbox address he had given her. Once a year he would visit her in Devon, the week of her birthday, for two days. Preferring always to stay at a local hotel rather than at her home. With each minute revelation, my father grew increasingly uncomfortable and began to usher her away from personal details towards logistics. His respect for Mr Mason's privacy superseded his curiosity and for that he was a far better man than I.

Today, just as I arrived, a car filled with boxes pulled away. In the twelve years since my father had handed Mr Mason the keys I had never been back inside.

To my surprise, Mr Mason had barely changed the furnishings which meant the whole place still carried the unmistakeable touch of my mother. From the banisters she had painted yellow, to the tiny shelf she had built just for her radio, to the plum curtains my parents had bickered over. She had made the mistake of insisting we all go to pick them, bribing me with the promise of iced buns and my father with his favourite delight, a bargain. It had been a grey day of traffic and rain but it was when my father had to park on a meter that darkness really descended. He stood sullen as she debated between cream or green or plum and I sneaked off to get my iced buns. Returning quickly with four instead of three and, the best bit, still warm. Looking between her moody husband and greedy son she quickly decided to opt for plum. With ten minutes left on the meter, we sat in the car eating our sticky buns. As it turned out my mother's curtains had outlasted both her and Mr Mason.

As I stand in Mr Mason's room touching the curtains, I finally begin to digest what my father said about the cause of death being cancer, so he knew. He wanted to be here when it happened.

Independent.

At home.

'Kabir, Kabiiiiiiiiiiiiiiir.' my father calls from the kitchen.

'Coming.'

As I enter he holds out a Seasons Greetings card. I recognise the cover.

'It was stuck on the cupboard. His family must have left it.'

I look at a few markings on the cabinets where others must have been.

As I open it I recognise my writing. I had been trying my best to make it neat.

Dear Mr Mason,

Wishing you a Merry Christmas and Happy New Year. Please let me know if the new boiler causes any issues.

> Best wishes,
> Mr Aziz and family

It was from last year, a few months before my mother died. My father tucked it into his jacket pocket.

'The builders are coming on Monday so if you want any of her things take them now.'

I can't answer.

'Have a think.'

'No, they're his things. He looked after them. I can't. '

'You sure?'

'Yes.'

Suddenly desperate to get out, 'Can we go for iced buns?'

'Now?'

'Please.'

About the authors

The Whole Kahani is a collective of British fiction writers of South Asian origin. The group formed in 2011 to provide a creative perspective that straddles cultures and boundaries both emotional and geographical. Its aim is to give a new voice to old stories and increase the visibility of South Asian writers in Britain.

Mona Dash was born in Odisha, India, and settled in London in 2001. With a background in Engineering and Management, she works in Telecoms Solution Sales. She writes fiction and poetry and her work has been and anthologised internationally. She has gained a Masters in Creative Writing, with distinction, from the London Metropolitan University. She is currently working towards a PhD in Area Studies. 'Dawn-drops' (Writer's Workshop, India) is her first collection of poetry. 'Untamed Heart' (Tara Research India Press) is her first novel.
Website: www.monadash.net

Kavita A. Jindal is the author of 'Raincheck Renewed', published to critical acclaim by Chameleon Press. Her story 'A Flash of Pepper' won the Vintage Books/Foyles 'Haruki Murakami competition' in 2012. Her work has appeared in literary journals, anthologies and newspapers around the world. Kavita was born and raised in India and has lived in both Hong Kong and England for many years. She is a Senior Editor at the Asia Literary Review.
Website: www.kavitajindal.com
Twitter: @writerkavita

Rohan Kar was born in London, but spent his early years in Sri Lanka. Several of his short stories have been published in anthologies (Fish, The New Writer, MIR, Tindal Street Press) and, in 2005, he was a winner of the Scottish Open International Poetry awards with his poem, Seeing True, about a father's fear for his son in war. He studied at the Universities of Kent, London and Harvard, and graduated from Birkbeck College's Creative Writing MA with distinction. Rohan has worked as an engineer, trade journalist, lawyer and teacher.

Radhika Kapur When she's not writing fiction, Radhika works in advertising and her work has won accolades at advertising festivals such as Cannes, One Show, Clio and Asia-Pacific Adfest. Her writing has been published by The Pioneer and the Feminist Review, amongst others. She recently won third place at a European screenwriting competition and is currently working on a feature film script.

Dimmi Khan is a graduate of the London School of Economics and has Masters Degrees in Islamic Studies, Information Systems and Creative Writing. He also has a lifelong passion for archaeology, human evolution, ancient history and Bollywood. He is a published short story writer and novelist, and is the co-author of *When Ali Met Honour* (Dahlia Publishing, 2015).
Twitter: @dimmikhan

Shibani Lal was born in Bombay and moved to the UK in 2000. After a brief stint in Singapore and Paris, she currently

lives in London, and works in the City. Shibani writes poetry and short stories. Her story "A Cup of Tea" was adjudged runner-up in the 2015 Asian Writer Prize.
Many of her stories draw upon her own experiences of cross-cultural relationships, family ties as well as exploring themes of love, loss and displacement.

C. G. Menon is the 2015 winner of the Asian Writer short story prize, The Short Story award and the Winchester Writers Festival short story prize. Her work has been broadcast on radio and is published or forthcoming in a number of journals and anthologies, including The Lonely Crowd, the Willesden Herald anthology, Siren Press' Fugue II and two of the Words and Women prize anthologies. She currently splits her time between London and Cambridge, and is working on her first novel.
Website: https://cgmenon.wordpress.com/
Twitter: @cg_menon

Iman Qureshi Iman's first play 'Speed' was produced by Kali Theatre at the Tristan Bates Theatre, and her short film is currently being developed by B3 Media. She is a member of Tamasha playwrights - a writer led collective affiliated with Tamasha Theatre. Iman has also written for a number of publications including the Guardian, Independent, Huffington Post, Time Out, and spoken on BBC Radio networks around issues relating to race and sexuality. She was shortlisted for the Muslim Writer's Award 2011, and the Allen Wright Award for features in 2010.

Reshma Ruia is the author of 'Something Black in the Lentil Soup'. It was described in the Sunday Times as 'a gem of straight-faced comedy.' Her second novel, 'A Mouthful of Silence,' was shortlisted for the 2014 SI Leeds Literary Prize. Her short stories and poems have appeared in various International anthologies and magazines such as 'Too Asian, Not Asian Enough,' and also commissioned for Radio 4. She has a PhD and Masters with Distinction in Creative Writing and post graduate and undergraduate degrees from the London School of Economics. Born in India, but brought up in Italy, her narrative portrays the inherent tensions and preoccupations of those who possess multiple senses of belonging.
Twitter: @reshmaruia

Farrah Yusuf was born in Pakistan and brought up in London. She writes plays, short stories and is currently working on her first novel. She took part in Kali Theatre TalkBack (2014/2015) and the Royal Court Theatre (2015) playwriting groups. Her short stories have been published in Five Degrees: The Asian Writer Short Story Prize (2012), SADAA Against the Grain (2013) and Beyond the Border (2014) anthologies and shortlisted for the Writeidea Short Story Prize (2014 and 2015).
Website: www.farrahyusuf.com